S U F F
FOLK
TALES

SUFFOLK
FOLK TALES

KIRSTY HARTSIOTIS

The
History
Press

To my parents,
Cherry and David Wilkinson

First published 2013
Reprinted 2013, 2016

The History Press
The Mill, Brimscombe Port
Stroud, Gloucestershire, GL5 2QG
www.thehistorypress.co.uk

British Library Cataloguing in Publication Data.
A catalogue record for this book is available from the British Library.

ISBN 978 0 7524 6747 4

Typesetting and origination by The History Press
Printed in Great Britain

CONTENTS

ACKNOWLEDGEMENTS

There are many people to thank in the creation of this book. Special thanks go to Heather and Peter Phillips for assistance with 'The Silly Saints', to Tony Matthews with the Blyford ghosts and to Jude Avery and Robin Ellis with 'The Bells of Minsmere'. I'd also like to thank Sue and Roger Freeman, Gabby Ballantine, Vic Harrup, June Brereton and David Phelps for the loan of books and help with locations. Thanks go to Dr Monika Simon for translating, from the Latin, Ralph of Coggeshall's three Suffolk wonder tales, and for information on Hugh Bigod, and to Monika and her father Dr Helmut Simon for the German translation in 'Guardian of the Breckland'.

I'd like to thank Valerie Dean, Fiona Eadie, Mark Hassell, Diana Humphrey, Austin Keenan, Kevan Manwaring, David Phelps, Karola Renard and Glenn and Mags Smith for listening to and commenting on these Suffolk stories. As always, I am very grateful for the unceasing support and love from my wonderful husband Anthony Nanson, who listened to and discussed stories, donated his superb copy-editing skills and visited many sites with me. But it is my parents, to whom this book is dedicated, who deserve the greatest thanks. Cherry and Dave Wilkinson were behind the project one hundred and ten per cent, offering local knowledge, finding contacts, helping with research and giving me support when I needed it most. They also visited many sites, through sun and rain and snow, taking me all around our county during the course of my research. I am so grateful to them, and I hope that it was as fun for them as it was for me.

MAP OF THE STORIES

ILLUSTRATIONS

The cover illustration is by Katherine Soutar. The map and line drawings are by the author (© 2013). All other illustrations are from the Dover Pictorial Archive and are reproduced in accordance with their terms and conditions.

INTRODUCTION

'Suffolk has hardly any stories.' That was the suggestion from both books and people when I first investigated the tales of my home county. Suffolk folk, some books alleged, were too pragmatic for fairy tales. Either that or they were not willing to talk to strangers about what they knew. Having grown up in East Anglia, I knew that this wasn't true. We lived just three miles from where Maria Marten was murdered. I remember being fascinated by the swan my mum made for a theatrical production of 'The Green Children'. My parents were – and are – heavily involved in the county's vibrant folk scene, and I witnessed Morris dancing and mummers' plays around the county. There were stories of Black Shuck and witches. As a student I became intrigued by Suffolk's Anglo-Saxon and medieval tales. The county possesses two of England's most famous folktales: 'Cap' o' Rushes' and 'Tom Tit Tot', and many other tales. Indeed, it was hard to choose which stories to include in this selection of thirty tales. Suffolk abounds with stories, and its people are still creating tales to explain the unexplainable.

Who are the South Folk? Before the Romans came, the territory of Suffolk was home to the British tribes of the Trinovantes and the Iceni. Suffolk came into being with the arrival of the Anglo-Saxons. They probably arrived during the Roman period, as settlers on what became known as the Saxon Shore. By the seventh century, East Anglia's King Raedwald – who may have been buried in the richest Anglo-Saxon burial ground ever found in Britain, Sutton Hoo – was overlord of all the English. The last of Raedwald's line was King Edmund, who became England's patron saint. Of Suffolk's two county towns, Ipswich and Bury St Edmunds, the former was the county's main trading port and the latter the home of one of England's richest abbeys. By the Middle Ages, Suffolk was one of the wealthiest and most populous counties in England. The wool trade brought prosperity to a growing middle class, and a slew of impressive churches and houses were built with wool money. When the wool trade ceased, Suffolk fell back on farming and fishing and embraced puritan values. Today, Suffolk still has a primarily rural economy: huge fields of crops dominate the low-lying landscape and the coast is now mainly dedicated to tourism and wildlife.

I've tried to present a diverse spread of tales. The Anglo-Saxons and Middle Ages are well represented with kings, saints and Ralph of Coggeshall's wonder tales. Later on come smugglers and fishermen. The impact of World War II on the county's imagination is also explored.

There are many distinct areas in Suffolk, so I wanted to ensure that I represented as many as I could. Until 1974 Suffolk comprised two administrative counties, West and East Suffolk. The east is dominated by the sea and abounds with tales of merfolk, Vikings, smugglers, sunken towns and black dogs. In contrast, the west is alive with fairies, religion, doomed romances and the trials and tribulations of farming folk.

It has been a voyage of rediscovery for me to revisit familiar places and see them with new eyes. I have tried to visit all of the locations of the tales and to evoke their sense of place. Suffolk's landscape gets accused of being nothing but flat. In reality, it is a varied landscape. The rolling hills and chocolate-box buildings of the south. The sandy Breckland in the northwest. The many rivers, from the Waveney to the Stour. The heavy soil of High Suffolk. Coastal marsh and heath and the eroding sea. Many stories take place in the wilder reaches of the county – in the marshes, the Brecks, the heathlands, woods and on the coast. However, the denizens of folktales haunt the villages and towns as well. In fact, the county's fairy folk are resolutely urban. Their favourite place is right in the middle of Stowmarket!

Many stories were already well shaped; these I have simply retold in my own words. Others in this book I composed from the myriad local legends and fragments of tales I have found. I have prioritised stories with imaginative or supernatural elements and mostly avoided stories that are simply tales from history. You will not find the familiar tales of witchcraft here. If there is one thing that Suffolk folk believed in, it was witches. This belief led to a sad period in the county's history. From the sixteenth to the nineteenth century, numerous women and men were accused of witchcraft and put on trial. Many lost their lives. The worst period was in the seventeenth century, thanks to the efforts of the self-styled Witchfinder General, Matthew Hopkins. These real-life tales of superstition and intolerance should certainly be told, so that we remember this dark period in the county's history. But these historical tales, I felt, didn't have a place in this selection of folktales. Instead you'll find cunning folk and a famous wizard, to represent more positively the county's fascination with magical people.

It is my hope that these tales will help to recapture the sense of place that we are rapidly losing in our modern world. My family were incomers to the county in the early 1970s, and we have all actively gone out to discover the stories of our adopted county. I encourage you to visit the locations of the stories, experience the tales in their settings and then, perhaps, tell them yourself, to help ensure that the stories will never be forgotten.

ONE

THE GREEN
CHILDREN

During the reign of King Stephen, Aylwin and Elstan of Woolpit were on their way through the woods to check their snares. They knew they had to be careful with their footing in this part of the wood, as there were pits in the claggy ground and blocks of old brick to trip over. The place was snarled with brambles and nettles; hardly a proper wood at all. No one came here, as it was said to be infested with wolves. Ideal for poaching.

That day they made their way up the slope about a mile from Woolpit, on the way to Elmswell. One snare held a young hare, which pleased them, but the rest were empty. Then Elstan caught a movement out of the corner of his eye.

'Get out your sling,' he whispered. 'There's something there.'

The two of them crept forward, further up the hill towards Elmswell, Alywin with his sling at the ready, until the ground suddenly dipped into a large bramble-filled pit. Elstan slipped, skidded and fell, and a scream filled the air.

A child's scream.

They peered into the pit, and there, huddled among the brambles, were two children. The children were dressed in rough homespun like themselves, but there the similarity ended. These children were green from their thick hair down to their bare toes.

Aylwin and Elstan froze. Green was an unlucky colour, a fairy colour. But these were just children. The older, a girl, looked to be about nine or ten years, the boy several years younger. They were scratched and weeping, and didn't look like a threat.

'Who are you?' asked Elstan. 'How did you get here? Where are your folks?'

The children stared back at him, and the men realised that they couldn't understand English. So Aylwin waded down into the pit and picked them up. They didn't fight; just wept some more.

Back in Woolpit, the whole village turned out to see the wonder. It was soon decided that they couldn't keep the children in Woolpit. Who would feed them? And would their landlord, the Abbot at Bury, approve of the ungodly things? Better to take them to someone who would find amusement in their novelty.

It was decided they should go to Sir Richard de Calne at Bardwell, eight miles away. He was the Constable of the Hundred, and would know what to do. Aylwin and Elstan were volunteered to take them. It was a long trek for the children. They wept as the men chivvied them on, step by step, until they came to the edge of Bardwell.

There were three manors in Bardwell. Unsure where to go, the Woolpit men went first to Wyken Hall. The servants there drove them away with fleas in their ears. Past Bardwell Hall they went, until at last they saw the squat tower of the church on a low hill ahead of them, and right beside it, the manor house of Wikes.

Sir Richard received the green children with grave thanks and gave Aylwin and Elstan some coins to see them on their way.

'You'll see them treated right, my lord?' asked Aylwin. 'Them's just children, when all's said and done.'

'No harm will come to them here,' said Sir Richard.

The children were brought before him, tear and travel stained. They really were very green. But it was only fair to try to communicate with them. He knew that the villagers would only have their own English, so he tried his Norman-French, and when that didn't work he tried a few words of Flemish. Neither had any effect, save to make the children cry even more.

His wife, Sibylla, leaned forward and whispered, 'Perhaps the poor mites are hungry. You can be sure those villeins wouldn't have given them anything from their stores.'

So bread and cider and good meat were set before them. But the children just stared at the spread as if it was poison. Even when Lady Sibylla tore off some bread and ate it herself to give them the idea, the children just wept. The lord and lady looked at each other. Unspoken between them was the thought that this newly brought marvel would not last that long.

Just at that moment, a maid came in from the gardens with baskets of broad beans, and as she walked past, both the children sat up and pointed.

'Bring those beans here,' cried Lady Sibylla, and she handed the basket to the children.

Immediately the children started pulling at the beans, but instead of trying to open the pods, they opened the stems. When they saw that they were empty, the tears started again. Lady Sibylla took the pods and snapped them open to reveal the beans inside. As soon as they saw the beans, both the children gave cries of joy and started to stuff the raw beans in their mouths.

After that, they settled into the household. Sir Richard saw to
it that while they were set simple tasks by the servants, they also
received instruction in English and French. He made the priest
their tutor, as they seemed to have no knowledge of God.

The girl thrived under this care. Her long green hair and green
skin soon glowed with health, and she was soon speaking a few
simple words to make her needs known. The boy was different.
After the bean harvest was over, the girl began to eat other things
– vegetables at first, then bread, although she would never touch
meat. But the boy wouldn't eat. His sister tried to tempt him with
all sorts of dainties that the kitchen staff gave her, but he just
turned away. She tried taking him out just before sunrise and just
after sunset, and that pleased him a little, but he shied away from
the bright sunshine. Soon enough he was too sick to go out, and
before harvest time was over he was dead.

Lady Sibylla spoke quietly to the priest, and he was buried
outside the west end of the church, with the other unbaptised
babes, to catch what holiness he could. His sister seemed grateful,
but it was hard to tell.

The girl would walk out from the manor whenever she could,
wandering over the Black Bourn and through the reed beds and
the stubbly fields. All the field hands knew to watch her, in case
she strayed too far, but she never did. She would come back with
bunches of the harvest flowers; loosestrife, mallow and dead-
nettles, take them to the little grave, and sit there quiet and alone.

By Christmas, her English and French were good and she
happily ate anything that was put in front of her. She went less
to the grave and was soon at the heart of the household, laughing
with the servants, playing rowdy games with the other children
and even flirting a little with Sir Richard's pages. Sir Richard
noticed, too, that the greenness of her skin had faded a little and
her hair had gained yellow tints. The marvel might soon be gone,
so he gathered his friends together for a great Christmas feast and
brought the girl out.

There were gasps of fear from his friends, and Sir Richard realised how used he was to her strangeness. She didn't seem worried

by the crowd. When he drew her forward to speak, she stepped up on the dais without any fear.

'Tell us, child, how you came here,' he asked. 'Tell us of your own home.'

The girl lifted her gaze to the assembled nobles. 'My brother and I were herding our father's sheep that day. Our land isn't like yours, but we do herd and farm like you do. I did this every day, but he was new to it, being young. One of our lambs got lost, and we set out after it. We could hear him bleating, so we just kept on going until we were far from our home. It was coming on for night when we found him, and when we turned to go back we realised we didn't know the way. So we just walked and walked, and then, in the darkness, we both fell, and we plummeted down a long way until we landed on dry earth and saw a tunnel stretching out. There were strange sounds all around us, sweet sounds, the like of which we'd never heard before, and those sounds drew us. We walked towards them. It seemed me that we walked all night. At last, we saw that there was light ahead, and we ran, hoping we'd be near our home, but as we came out the light was so bright that we both fell down in a faint. When we woke up those men were there, and they dragged us out, and it was so bright, and so strange, and we couldn't understand them at all.

'Our land isn't like yours. Yours is so bright! I find it lovely now, the sunshine on the flowers, but at home the sun is always beyond – just a distant glow to the west. Like twilight, it is a gentle, quiet light. We're all green. To see you pink people was a shock, but now it makes me laugh! And we would never eat the flesh of animals. It goes against all that is right. Our sheep were our friends; they gave us their wool so that we might be warm. But here everything is different. You have God to guide you – and the beautiful sound of the church bells that drew us here. Maybe it was God's plan to bring us here … but' – she glanced guiltily at Sir Richard – 'sometimes I wonder if I went back to Woolpit I might find my way home.'

Her words were a sensation. No one talked of anything else for a season. But soon new stories came to take the place of the marvel. The girl began to change as well. She was baptised, and given a name: Agnes. Slowly, as the season passed from winter into spring and from spring into summer, her greenness dwindled away, until her skin was simply pale and her hair simply fair. Those who came seeking the green child went away disappointed.

But Sir Richard remembered what she had said. So he had his men take her to Woolpit. The two farmers, Aylwin and Elstan, were fetched, and they showed the girl where they had found her. But though the brambles were cleared, there was nothing to be seen there but heavy clay. After that, Agnes never mentioned her first home again. She threw herself into the life of Wikes Manor and seemed to want to forget her origins.

Sir Richard saw that, though she was baptised, there were some things that made her different. She still liked to wander alone by the stream at sunset. More worryingly, she was drawn to the young men and seemed to see nothing wrong in exchanging kisses with his squires. It was disruptive, and he worried that there would soon be a shame she couldn't hide. With one of the lads, from Lynn in Norfolk, Sir Richard thought there was something more serious than just the flirting, so he gave Agnes a fine dowry, and she was married.

Agnes lived the rest of her life in Lynn, and gave birth to several children. None of them was green, but it was said that her descendants were all fun-loving and didn't fear God as much as they should.

This is perhaps Suffolk's most famous story and has been much written about. It comes from Ralph of Coggeshall, the sixth abbot of Coggeshall Abbey in Essex, who is best known for his work the Chronicon Anglicanum. *Of his tales, three of them are set in Suffolk. There are many theories about why the children were green and couldn't speak English. Were they the children of Flemish weavers? Did they walk through tunnels like those at Grimes Graves? Did they have an iron deficiency that produced anaemia? Or maybe they were simply from that other world.*

TWO

FIVE SKEINS A DAY

There was once a woman who baked five pies, enough for the week; but she forgot them in the oven. When she took them out, they were rock hard. She was a busy woman, so she called her daughter over and told her to put them in the pantry to let them come again. Her daughter, a lazy lass of sixteen, was amazed to hear that her mum could bake magic pies. She took them to the pantry, but even though they were rock hard, they smelt really good.

She thought to herself, 'If they will come again, I might as well eat them now.'

So she did.

Later, when her mum came in hungry after working, she asked her daughter to fetch her one of the pies, 'As surely they'll have come again by now'.

The girl trotted back to the pantry, but there wasn't a single pie come back again. She went back and told her mum so.

'Are you sure?' said her mother, shrugging. 'I'm hungry; I'll have one anyway.'

Her daughter stared at her.

'You can't – I ate them all, so you'll just have to wait for them to come again.'

Her mother was furious. Had the girl learnt nothing? Surely *everyone* knew that when a pie 'came again', the pastry was just sof-

tening in the air? She took her spindle and sat outside, still fuming.
As she span, a little song came to her.

'My daughter ate five pies today, five pies.'

She repeated it over and over. It began to ease her anger. Just a little.

As she was sitting there spinning and singing, the King happened to come past on his fine horse. He overheard the woman
singing, but couldn't quite catch the words.

'My good woman, what are you singing?'

The woman, embarrassed to be caught singing about her daughter's stupid gluttony, quickly changed the rhyme: 'My daughter
spun five skeins today, five skeins.'

The King was impressed. His mother had been a great spinner
and weaver, so he knew a little about such things.

'I've never heard of anyone who could do that. Show me this
daughter of yours.'

The girl was brought out, and the King looked her up and
down. She was as pretty as only sixteen can be; plump-cheeked
and rosy, her figure not yet showing what five pies a day can do.
The King smiled at her.

'I'll make you a bargain,' he said. 'Marry me, and for eleven
months you'll have everything you want: fine food, fine clothes
and as many servants as you like. But in the twelfth month you'll
spin me five skeins a day, and I'll cut off your head if you don't.'

The girl wasn't very impressed with this, and was just about to
open her mouth to refuse when her mother pulled her aside.

'Don't you do another foolish thing today! You say yes, and
sure as sure with a young bride in his bed he'll forget all about
them five skeins.'

So the girl said yes. She was taken to the palace, and before
she could turn round she was the Queen. It was fabulous: there
was fine food and clothes and servants, just as he'd said – and
the King himself wasn't so bad, either. She soon forgot about the
five skeins.

Eleven months is a long time when you are sixteen, but soon
enough they passed. On the evening before the beginning of the
twelfth month, the King took hold of his wife's hand and led her

up to a part of the castle she'd never been to before, high up in a tall tower. There, at the very top, was a small room with a barred window and nothing in it save a stool, a straw pallet for sleeping, a chamber pot – and a spinning wheel.

'My love, I've kept you well these last months, kept up my side of things, and now it's your turn,' said the King. 'Tomorrow, I'll bring you up some flax, and you'll spin me five skeins a day. If you don't – well, it's off with your head.'

Before she could say or do anything, he was out of the door. She heard the key turn in the lock, then heard his boots clattering down the stairs and away. The young Queen stood there in the little room and felt terror rise within her. In all those months of having fun she'd never even thought to learn to spin. She was certain her head would be off by the end of tomorrow. She sank down on the stool and wept.

How long she wept she didn't know, but after a while she became aware of a little scratching sound at the window. She went to have a look, and there was a strange little creature, all black from head to claw and with a whippy black tail.

'What're you crying for?' it asked.

Although she was foolish, the Queen wasn't a complete idiot. She could guess what the creature must be, and she knew to be cautious.

'What's it to you?' she said.

'Never you mind,' said the creature, with a pointy toothed smile. 'You just tell me.'

'It won't do me any good,' she said.

'You never know,' said the creature.

It came to the Queen that it wouldn't do any harm to tell – at least, no more harm than having her head chopped off tomorrow. So out poured the story of the five pies, and the five skeins, and the head chopping and all.

At the end of it the creature said, 'That's easily done. Let me come to your window at daybreak and give me the flax, and I'll have five skeins ready for you at sunset.'

But the Queen was still suspicious. 'What's your pay?'

The creature gave her a long, long look. 'I think you know. But I'll give you a chance. If you can guess my name before the month is out, then you can consider it all a gift. I'll be generous and give you three guesses a night – but if you can't guess right, well, you'll have to come along with me.'

The Queen sat back down on the stool and thought. It came to her that a month was a lot better than a day, and that three times thirty guesses was a lot of names.

So she said yes.

Both the King and the creature were as good as their word. Before dawn, a pile of flax was brought to her door with some stale bread and water. At daybreak the creature appeared at the window and spirited the flax away.

It was a long day, with nothing to do but think. By the end of the day the Queen had convinced herself that the creature wasn't coming back, and that her head would be off. But, just as the sun was setting, there was a scratching at the window and there was the creature with five beautifully spun skeins.

Then the game was on.

'What's my name?'

'Is it Bill?' she tried.

'No, it ain't!' cried the creature and twirled its whippy tail.

'Is it Mark?'

'No.'

It wasn't Ned either, and with that the creature was gone.

The next moment the door opened and there was her husband. He took up the skeins and examined them with delight.

'Well, it looks like I won't have to kill you today, my love – but there's always tomorrow.'

The next day was just the same. The flax was delivered; the creature took it away at dawn, and brought it back beautifully spun at sunset. Again the Queen tried three names, and again they were wrong, and then her husband appeared, praised her and threatened her in the same breath, and with that the day was over and she collapsed onto the pallet and slept.

The whole month went by in the same fashion. Each night the creature looked more and more gleeful, until there were just two days to go. When she sent it off that morning it was twirling its tail round and round and grinning.

To make things worse, she was running out of names. But that night she tried again.

'It is Nicodemus? Is it Samuel? It is Methusalem?'

But it was none of them, and the creature twirled its tail faster and faster. It looked at her with eyes like cold fire and said, 'Woman, there's only tomorrow left, and then you'll be mine.'

The Queen knew it was the end, but what could she do?

Her husband was as pleased with the skeins as ever. 'I'm sure there'll be skeins tomorrow night, so it looks like I won't have to kill you after all,' he said. 'You're as good as free for this year, so – why not – I'll take my supper with you!'

The supper was brought, and a comfortable chair for the King to sit on, and he tucked into his meal with gusto. After a while, though, he noticed that his wife barely picked at her food.

'Wife, you don't seem joyful that tomorrow we'll be reunited. You're not going to be all missy at me about our bargain, are you?'

The Queen shook her head. 'I'm just tired from all the spinning.'

'Well, let me tell you a tale to cheer you up. As I was out hunting today, I got separated from my friends and I rode into a place I'd never been before, an old chalk pit in the wood. Strange – I thought I knew every inch of my land. But stranger than that was thing that was in it. You'll never guess! It was a little black creature, sitting at a spinning wheel and spinning as fast – well, as you, my love – and it was singing its heart out as it worked.'

The Queen couldn't believe her ears. With her heart pounding in her ears, she asked, 'What was it singing?'

'Just some nonsense – "Nimmy nimmy not, my name is Tom Tit Tot!" Now isn't that the funniest thing?'

The Queen nearly fainted away, but she managed to smile.

The next day the flax was waiting as usual, and the creature came to fetch it.

'Last day,' it said.

'Last day,' agreed the Queen.

When the creature came back, he was grinning from ear to ear and twirling that whippy tail faster than ever.

Of course the Queen had an answer, but she was canny.

'Is it Solomon?'

Suddenly the creature was off the window sill and in the room, and there was the smell of sulphur everywhere.

'No!' it cried.

'Is it Zebedee?'

'No!' it cried, and came closer, almost close enough to touch. 'Last guess!'

The Queen edged away until her back was against the wall. She didn't have to try to look frightened as the creature approached. But, gathering her courage, she raised a shaky finger and cried, 'Nimmy nimmy not, your name is Tom Tit Tot!'

The creature gave a shrieking cry, and in a puff of fire and smoke was gone.

When her husband came in, she handed him the skeins.

'Well done, my love!' he cried. Then he smiled. 'Now you'll have nothing to worry about when you do it again next year.'

With that in mind, the Queen swallowed her pride. She went down to the village and asked her mother to teach her to spin. She soon became proficient, easily the best in the village thanks to her dedication. But she learnt that there was no way that anyone could spin five skeins a day, and she despaired.

Soon enough, though, she had something to take her mind off that next twelfth month. Nine months to the day after her release from the tower she gave birth to a beautiful baby girl. The King doted on the babe, and the Queen hoped that he would forget all about the skeins.

No such luck.

When the baby was only two months old, the King said it was time and that he would take her back to the tower to spin for her keep the day after tomorrow.

'You're not to worry,' he said. 'I'll bring the babe up to you every night, but if there aren't five skeins tomorrow, well, it's off with your head.'

The Queen knew there was no point in protesting, but she also knew the situation was hopeless. She went down to the kitchen door where no one would be watching, and she wept. It seemed that even the weather sympathised with her, as the heavens opened and a rainstorm thundered across the land.

While the rain poured down, the queen became aware of another sound, a knocking at the door. In her misery she ignored it at first, but it got more and more insistent. She got up and opened the door, and immediately a Gypsy woman bustled in, clutching baskets to her chest.

'I thought you were going to ignore me,' said the Gypsy, but then she looked closer at the Queen. 'I see that there is as much water in here as out there. Why are you weeping?'

The whole story poured out with the Queen's tears, of the five pies and Tom Tit Tot and her babe and her broken heart.

The Gypsy smiled. 'I think we can sort that once and for all.'

'What must I pay you?' rapped the Queen.

The Gypsy looked at her with sympathy and said, 'There now, don't you fear. All I want is a suit of fine clothes for my wedding on Monday morning.'

For a moment the Queen hesitated, as all her clothes came from the King, but then she thought that if she was dead by the end of the day after tomorrow she'd not care about a missing dress, and if she wasn't, well, she'd cross that bridge when she got there. She ran to her bedchamber and pulled out her best dress, some fancy shoes and jewels and shoved them into the Gypsy's arms.

'Just ask your husband to throw you a party tomorrow night, and I'll be there, and you shall see what you shall see.' And with that the Gypsy was off, with the fine clothes bundled up in her basket.

The King was only too happy to grant his wife her wish for a party to say farewell to her friends. The Queen dressed herself in her second-best dress, went down to the party and waited for the Gypsy woman.

The hours ticked by, and still the woman didn't come, and at midnight everyone was yawning and wanting to go off to their beds, but the Queen begged them to stay for just one more dance. As she spoke, in flounced the Gypsy woman, dressed in the Queen's finest and looking stunning. The King had his eyes on her at once.

'Who's this, my love?'

'Just a friend,' said the Queen, and drew the Gypsy aside.

The Gypsy woman smiled, and opened her pocket. Nestled inside was a clutch of eggs. As the Queen stared at them, the Gypsy cracked one, and a horrendous smell filled the air. Neither of them said anything, but after a while the strange smell started to fill the room, and people were backing away and looking accusingly at each other.

'What is that dreadful smell?' cried the King.

The Gypsy woman stepped forward and said, all apologetic, 'It's me, your Majesty.'

The King's eyes bulged.

'Well, get home and wash yourself!'

But the Gypsy shook her head.

'Your Majesty, washing won't do no good. It was the spinning what did it. When I was a lass I could spin four skeins a day and, well, my twatling bands broke and there's no helping it now. I hear your wife is a great spinner – quicker than me. Won't be long afore she stinks like I do.'

The Queen gave a burst of laughter, but the King didn't think it was funny at all. He turned to her and cried, 'Wife, if I ever see you spin again, I'll have your head!'

This is another well-known Suffolk tale, a version of the famous story of Rumpelstiltskin. It was told to Mrs Walter Thomas and her sister Lois Fison when they were children by their nurse, a West Suffolk lady. The story was published in Merry Suffolk: Master Archie and Other Tales, *in 1899, but the ending of the Gypsy woman section there was rather different. All the woman does is smear grease about and blame that on her spinning days. The true earthy Suffolk ending was revealed by the President of the Folklore Society, Edwin Sidney Hartland, in 1900.*

THREE

THE KING OF ALL THE ANGLES

Late in 1937, Dorothy Cox stared out of the first-floor window of her friend May Pretty's house at Sutton Hoo. Far off, down the hill, she could see the River Deben moving slowly from Woodbridge to the sea. Closer in lay the woodland, the cedar trees dark above the misty meadow where the mound lay. She leaned against the side of the window, her mind only half on what she was looking at, the other half on her old friend's struggles in her widowhood to bring up her young son. Then something caught her eye. Around the big mound was a circle of men. For a moment, Dorothy thought they must be intruders, but then she saw that they carried shields and spears, and she realised that, once again, she was looking into the beyond. She watched them circling round and round in the rising mist until they were gone and only the very top of the dark cedar was visible.

She didn't say anything to May at first, but each time she came to stay she saw the figures in their solemn circle. Early the next year, she broached the subject with her.

'I think they're trying to tell us something. I think they're protecting something precious. Didn't you say that people thought there were kings buried there?'

May smiled.

'Everyone knows that the mounds were robbed out centuries ago. What an imagination you have, Dorothy!'

But Dorothy was sure, and pressed May to get an archaeologist to look at the site. May shook her head; she had enough to worry about without thinking about dead kings. But after that conversation she couldn't get the warriors out of her head. One night, she dreamed that she saw a funeral procession, women weeping and wailing, the richly dressed figure of a man in a golden helmet carried to the ship in the waiting mound, the priest raising his arms to invoke the gods...

She awoke in a sweat at dawn and rushed to the window.

There, standing on the mound, was a warrior dressed in strange clothes and wearing a golden helmet that glinted in the washed-out light as the white mist rose up around him.

Raedwald, King of the East Angles, a proud Wuffinga, descend-ant of Woden and Caesar, stood in his temple in Rendlesham and looked around him with pleasure. This great raftered hall with the light filtering in from the smoke holes contained two powerful altars. One, blood stained, was made of ash wood, carved with wolves and ravens, where fierce Woden stood, gold-covered, fixing him with his one eye. The other altar was lit by a tended flame. A cross stood on an embroidered cloth and an Irish bowl hung above, glinting in the candlelight, waiting to be filled in the mass. Strong gods, of vengeance and mercy, to protect his home and kingdom. The scent of incense and sharp herbs soothed his senses. He inhaled deep, closed his eyes and remembered his dark initiation into the lore of his ancestor, and the harsh slap of the cold North Sea as Bishop Mellitus dunked him under the waves and baptised him for Christ.

'My lord King!'

Raedwald turned to see a travel-stained young man at the entrance. The man's eyes flashed with fear at the idol and the cross, but he walked towards Raedwald and knelt.

'Sire, there is a stranger at our borders. Athelfrith's brother-in-law, the exile Prince Edwin, has left his Mercian wife and run from Athelfrith to claim your sanctuary.'

Raedwald glanced back at the altars, at cunning Woden and gentle Christ. Had it come at last, his chance to take the other Kingdoms of the Angles under his lordship? What blood would be spilled from the words he was to utter?

'Then what are you waiting for?' he said. 'Bring him to Rendlesham, where we will feast the rightful King of Northumbria!'

So Edwin came to East Anglia and found at last a safe haven from the man who had stolen his kingdom, forced his sister into marriage, hounded him from his fosterage in Gwynedd and then from sanctuary in Mercia, where his wife and sons still waited. Raedwald and his queen received Edwin with honour and affection and Raedwald's son Raegenere became like a brother to him. Together they plotted how they would snatch the throne of Northumbria from the usurper.

It was not to last. Only a few short weeks had passed when Raedwald received the first messenger from the north.

'Athelfrith will give you gold if you kill his kinsman.'

Kill an honoured guest in his hall? One to whom he had offered guest-rights? Raedwald sent the messenger home with a rejection ringing in his ears.

Again a messenger came, with the same message and the offer of more gold.

Once more Raedwald refused.

Then a group of warriors came. Their message from Athelfrith was different.

'If you do not kill my kinsman Edwin, then I will bring the killing to you. I will bring war to your kingdom, crush you and your paltry sons beneath my heel; make the East Angles my own.'

Raedwald listened to the message in silence. This was the moment. The decision he made now would allow him to seize the overlordship of South and North – or fail, and die, and leave his kingdom in foreign hands. His memories of battle flooded back. Pain. Death. Blood. Rape. The burning of settlements. Could he bring this on his people? Maybe it was better to sacrifice the stranger for the good of his farmers and thanes. Maybe it was better to be satisfied with his own kingdom than to lose it all for ambition. In a secret meeting with his thanes, he agreed that he would kill Edwin. Then, doubt and guilt clawing at him, he strode to his temple and fell down in front of his altars to pray for guidance.

The gods were silent.

Raedwald's meeting hadn't been as secret as he thought. His own son, Raegenere, was torn between loyalty to his father and to his friend; but what his father had done was not honourable. He made his way outside the Great Hall to where Edwin sat, staring out into the dark woods that surrounded the hall.

'Edwin,' he cried. 'You must leave!' He told him what his father planned to do. 'But don't despair. Let's leave now, this very minute. I know the land. I can take you to a place of safety among my mother's kin in Essex.'

Edwin was deeply moved that Raegenere should go against his father to save him, but he knew he could not go. He had long accepted that it was time to stop running, time to stand and fight. In truth there was nowhere left to run, despite his friend's brave words.

So he thanked Raegenere and said, 'Your father has offered me no harm. I can't betray that friendship by fleeing. And if I must die, then I would rather he killed me than one less noble.'

Raegenere bowed his head. Unable to bear what was going to happen, he strode back to the hall.

Edwin stayed outside watching the stars with a heavy heart. How long he sat there, he did not know, but when it was so late that the moon was setting behind the dark trees, a figure emerged from the darkness, a man wearing a long robe and with a circle of hair cut from the centre of his scalp. A man who glowed around the edges of his body.

Edwin jumped back with fear, but the man raised a hand to quiet him and said, 'Why do you sit here alone when all are sleeping in Raedwald's hall?'

'What business is it of yours?' cried Edwin.

The man smiled, and with his smile Edwin felt peace spread over him and he sank back down. The man told him that he knew who he was and why he sat outside, alone. Then he asked Edwin, 'What reward would you give to one who would deliver you from the evil that surrounds you?'

'I would give anything in my power.'

'What would you do if you were delivered so far as to become the most powerful king in the land?'

'Nothing would stop my gratitude.'

A third time the man spoke, asking Edwin, 'Will you follow the guidance of the one who delivers to you all I have described?'

'Of course.'

The man laid his right hand on Edwin's forehead and said, 'When you receive this sign, you will know that the time to fulfil your promise has come.'

Then he vanished.

Inside the temple, at the same moment, Raedwald rose from his altars and left the building with an empty hollowness in his heart. Wearily he trudged to his chamber where his wife waited sleepless for his return.

He told her what she already knew: the secret meeting and his decision.

Anger flared in her face. 'Is it not unworthy of a great king to sell, for gold, his dear friend in his hour of need? Worse still to sacrifice your royal honour – most valuable of possessions – for money!'

Raedwald realised then that the gods had answered his prayer. He went straight back to Athelfrith's men with a message of war. Raegenere ran to Edwin and told him with great joy of his father's change of heart. Edwin thought on the words of the stranger, and he wondered.

Raedwald immediately gathered his army and marched north. He sailed across the Wash and marched swiftly through the Kingdom of Lindsey, gathering men from his vassal king as he went, until he had a mighty force.

Athelfrith raced south with his own army, and they clashed in a bitter, bloody battle at the ford on the River Idle near Littleborough.

The Idle ran red with the blood of the Angles that day, and great was the feast left for the wolf and the raven. Athelfrith died on that field, and Raedwald and Edwin were triumphant. But Raedwald left the battle deep in grief after the body of Raegenere was found among the slain. He buried his son with great honour on Ermine Street at Caenby, then marched north to York with Edwin. Raedwald was declared the King of all the Angles, but it was a hollow victory that had come at too great a cost.

Long did his queen weep when he told her of their son's death, but still she maintained that he had done the right thing to support Edwin. Raedwald knew in his heart that his doubt had caused his son's death. A punishment from the gods. But there was peace, and he had a second son. Eorpwald was trained to be king after his father. For ten peaceful years Raedwald was overlord of the North and the South. It was said that in that time a woman with a new-born babe could walk from one side of the country to another without fear.

At the end of those ten years, in 624, Raedwald died. The poets said that he had a good life and a good death. It fell to Eorpwald to bury his father, to bring the King's ship up the Deben, to build the mound around it, to place his father in the burial ground with all the honour of a son of Woden and a son of Christ. There they left him, on the banks of the river, to take his place alongside his thanes and his ancestors.

It was to Edwin that the mantle of overlordship fell. And one day, years later, the man from his vision walked into his court and laid a hand on Edwin's forehead. Bishop Paulinus brought Christianity to Northumbria, and it is said that Edwin sent a mission to his friends in East Anglia to show them the Way.

That morning, her vision still fresh in her mind, May Pretty sat down and wrote to the curator at Ipswich Museum, demanding that he send an archaeologist to excavate the mounds. The curator sent a local man, Basil Brown, to investigate, and May asked him to look at the mound that the ghosts had circled and on which her warrior had stood. But Basil showed her where the mound had been dug into.

'It's all robbed out. No point in digging there.'

He dug two other mounds that summer of 1938 – but they were empty.

He came back the next summer, but this time May prevailed and it was her mound, now prosaically called Mound One, that was scheduled to be dug.

It is well known what was discovered in that mound. The ghost of a great ship and, within it, the richest Anglo-Saxon burial ever found in England.

And on 3 September that year, 1939, Britain declared war on Germany. May gave Sutton Hoo over to the military, who used it as a training ground for military vehicles. When she thought of all that had happened, she often asked herself whether the spirits had somehow known that war and destruction was coming, that the king in the mound was reaching out across the ages that he might not be forgotten, that his legacy be kept safe.

The Sutton Hoo burials remain one of the most important and intriguing archaeological finds in British history. The grave in Mound One is indisputably the grave of a member of the ruling elite, and royal graves are vanishingly rare in archaeology. There is a strong case for thinking Raedwald was buried there. The date is about right, and he was the most powerful Wuffing king, Overlord of the Angles. He would have had the wealth and connections needed to amass such grave goods. Bede tells us Raedwald had Christian and pagan altars, and the burial does contain some Christian items. But, whoever was buried in Sutton Hoo's Mound One, the objects found there have a lasting appeal, thanks to their beauty, craftsmanship and richness. As a student I studied at York under Professor Martin Carver, who ran the Sutton Hoo excavation in the 1980s and 1990s. He arranged for his students to go to the British Museum and see the treasure first hand. We were allowed to handle the shoulder clasps, and I still class that as one of the most thrilling moments of my life.

FOUR

THE DEVIL
IN SUFFOLK

The Devil was feeling good. He'd just had a very profitable time in Cambridgeshire and he thought that he might dare to do something he rarely did: go into silly Suffolk. That didn't mean Suffolk was foolish, but rather that it was 'sele', holy. This time, the Devil felt confident he could make an impression, but he decided he would play it safe.

He'd heard that there was a wedding in Exning that day. The thing about Exning was that it was cut off from the rest of Suffolk, surrounded by a sea of Cambridgeshire. He'd give the Devil's own blessing to ensure the marriage was over before it began. He arrived in Exning in the guise of a man dressed in fine wedding clothes. Even in this small part of Suffolk he was nervous. He crept around the north side of the church. He'd sneak in the back and work his dark magic from there, incognito. But as he snuck round to the porch, he saw the bride's party coming up the path towards him.

He flung himself against the wall, but not before one of the bridesmaids spotted him. Although the Devil may think he looks like you and me, there's always something that gives him away. The bridesmaid let out an almighty shriek, and the Devil took fright. The whole congregation piled out of the church, and when they saw the Devil they gave chase. The Devil didn't wait; he fled out of the back gate, along Church Lane, following the stream, with the whole wedding party – bride, groom and guests – racing behind him.

He ran as far as Reach, in Cambridgeshire, and for moment he thought he would stay there. But he was furious, and the more he thought about it the more he wanted revenge. Suffolk would pay! He transformed himself back into the ole Devil with his cloven hooves and his horns and a flaming tail. He marched out back towards Suffolk, and as he went his tail dug into the ground and churned up the earth on either side so that a long ditch was formed from the edge of the fen to the forest at Woodditton – nearly back in Suffolk again. The walls of the ditch stood more than thirty foot high. They towered over the flatlands. Let the Suffolk folk try to get past that!

'I'll keep them and their holy ways trapped inside!'

That's how the Devil's Ditch was formed.

His revenge was waiting. As it was a church that had kept him out, the Devil decided he would destroy or change every church in Suffolk. He sniffed the air, then raced straight into the heart of the county. There he saw Stonham Aspal church tower. So tall it was, towering over everything around, that it made the Devil angry. How dare these folk be so pious! He'd take them down a peg or two.

That night, the Devil flicked his tail again. The top of the tower crashed to the ground. He was so angry that he trampled the stones into tiny pieces. The next morning the villagers came to church and saw half their tower gone, but a fine new stone path led up to the porch.

To this day, Stonham Aspal is the only place you have to walk over the tower to get into the church.

The Devil was pleased, but felt a little exposed there in the centre of the county, so he skulked to the border with Norfolk, the River Waveney. At Syleham he discovered the villagers actually building a church. They had got to about waist height. He could have some fun with this! He worked all night long.

The next morning the church was gone. The villagers scratched their heads and they searched for the stones. They found no sign of them. They headed over the bridge into Norfolk to look, and there might have been a diplomatic incident between Syleham and Brockdish that day if someone hadn't spotted the church upriver.

The villagers raced off. Sure enough, there was the church just as they'd left it – but now on a water meadow. Was it some strange practical joke? They carted the stones back to the original spot and started building the church back up again.

The Devil grinned. That night he took it all down again.

The next morning the villagers found the church back by the river, and once more they carted it back.

The Devil waited until the church was nearly complete, and then he acted again. The villagers couldn't believe it when they saw their church was gone once more, and they hot-footed it to the river. Sure enough, there was the church, but the Devil wasn't such a good builder as he thought. Not only was their lovely church in the wrong place, but it was all skew-whiff! The nave was tiny and low and the chancel huge. The villagers were furious, but there was nothing to be done. They said to each other that it was God's will and the church had to stay.

God's will? The Devil was pretty cross at that.

He stomped off to the Saints. He stopped at South Elmham St James and nipped inside the church. Everyone was out at harvest, and it was empty. Now what could he do? Almost immediately, he heard a shriek. He started, and saw a child at the door. The Devil never likes to be seen. He had to run! The child was in the only exit – or was she? There was a little door in the west, so he shot through it, only to find himself trapped in the bell tower. He cursed, and the stone gleamed hot.

Then he heard it: a clashing and a banging, like of a thousand pots and pans.

He climbed up the bell tower and peered out through the window. Below the tower was what looked like all the villagers, giving him the rough music. He could feel its anger coursing through him. Perhaps he'd tear down the tower, he thought, and burn them all!

Just as he thought that, the priest came running up.

'No, no, you fools! Don't give him the rough music! That's only making him stronger.' Then pointing at three strong men, he cried, 'You, you and you – get in there and start ringing the bells! The rest of you, put your hands together and pray!'

The Devil didn't dare move. The bell ringers came in, and the bells were rung until he was juddering inside and the prayers were causing his blood to boil. With a shout he smashed through the wall and was away. It's said that the scar in the tower has never healed.

The Devil didn't care; he just wanted to get away. He fled right down the county till he saw the Stour ahead and Essex beyond. Then he dug in his claws and turned himself about. Suffolk would not defeat him!

At East Bergholt he found them making a new tower, and he knew what to do. Down the tower came each night, until the villagers were tearing out their hair. But they were determined, and to the Devil's fury they began to build a wooden cage for their bells on the ground instead. Well, he wasn't having that, and was about to destroy the cage, when he felt a tug.

Thirty five miles north, at Westleton Church, someone was summoning the Devil.

'If you run seven times around the church, he'll be chained in the crypt and has to answer anything you ask of him!'

All the kids were cheering their friend on as she raced around the church – five times, six, seven times.

The Devil suddenly found himself in a dank crypt, chained to the wall at his ankles and his wrists, and there above him was a girl's grinning face.

'You have to answer my question! Will Bill invite me to the harvest horkey?'

The Devil rolled his eyes. He'd been pulled away for *this*?

He gave his answer, and was released. Now all he wanted to do was get out of Suffolk. He raced south, and as he raced through Eastbridge, the priest, John Neale, was sitting in the pub and he sensed something. The priest ran into the street, and there was the Devil. Neale thought fast. He whipped off his boot and began chanting. The Devil felt that pull again, and strained against it. But those prayers were too strong. He was sucked up and spat into a dark, smelly and slimy place – the priest's boot. Neale quickly tied up the top of the boot, shucked off his other shoe and ran down the path through the marshes, past the ruined monastery of the bells, and onto the beach. There he cast the boot out to sea.

The Devil went very still. He is made of hiss and steam, and if he's dunked in seawater, he'll be a long time recovering. So he waited, and for what seemed an eternity he felt the press of the water around him. After a long while he sensed that the water was no longer salt, but fresh, and then he was flying through the air and he landed with a thwack on something hard. As he lay there wondering what to do, he heard a voice.

'Just an old boot! Throw it back.'

No! The Devil burst out of the boot and swelled to his full size and looked down to see two terrified fishermen cowering on the deck of their boat. He looked around and saw that he was back at the River Stour, with Suffolk on the one side and Essex on the other. Without a second thought he leapt off the boat and into Essex, and it was a very long time before he dared come back into silly Suffolk.

> *The Devil often makes the landscape in stories, but that isn't true in Suffolk. Perhaps with a little less landscape to deal with, the stories have settled on the tall, prominent churches instead. Whatever happens, though, the Devil is always defeated and the church goes on.*

FIVE

THE REVENGE OF NAN BARRETT

Nan Barrett was the cunning woman of Eye. She lived all alone with her cat in a small cottage in the shadow of the old castle hill. Whatever Eye's vicar thought of the steady stream of people who went to Nan's door, he never said. As he went about his business, so did she. There had been cunning men and women in Eye since people first settled on the island, and, though Eye was an island no longer, the need for a cunning woman had not changed.

In those uncertain times, though, people were beginning to find new words for Nan: 'witch' they called her; 'hag', 'devil's apprentice'. Some folks would make the sign for evil as they passed her little pink cottage, and they'd whisper about ungodly doings and familiars. But there were more who shook their heads at the rumours. Women whose babes would not have been born live without Nan's sure touch, men whose pigs or sheep or cattle were cured by her calming words and potent potions, and, more than anything, those who had lost something, only to have Nan find it.

For Nan's real talent lay in finding what had been lost. She was renowned well beyond the town, and people would flock to her even from over the county border. Wedding rings were a speciality, and purses, and there was more than one child that had been found wailing in the marshes, thanks to a word or two from Nan.

Harmless enough; and Nan was very careful not to say anything other than kind words. She was certainly no fool and she could see well enough without her second sight that the tide was turning against the cunning folk. But for now, she was safe enough.

One day, there was a rap at her door, and a solid, well-dressed woman stepped under the low lintel into Nan's kitchen. Nan could see she was a farmer's wife, and that she didn't approve. All the little tells were there, from her stiff back to her sniffy expression, but Nan never turned anyone away if they had a legitimate request.

The goodwife was not convinced. She'd married into the area, and her own strict religious upbringing meant that to come to Nan's was a serious concession. But when profit was on the line, there was little choice. Besides, her milkmaids spoke so glowingly of the woman that she had to give her a try.

'You've lost something, then?' said Nan.

'A feather-bed's worth of goose feathers! Just disappeared overnight!'

Nan nodded sagely, and for a moment her eyes unfocused and she seemed to be looking far away. Then she said, 'There's one feeling guilty right now. Like as not, those feathers'll be waiting for you when you get home.'

The farmer's wife was pleased to hear this, but she was not impressed. No magic words? No heathen gestures? No potions or crystal ball? And already the old woman was stretching out a hand for payment for those few words!

'Anyone could say that! You've told me nothing – and nothing is what I'll give you!'

With that the goodwife turned and stalked to the door, but she froze with her hand on the latch as Nan's voice rang out behind her: 'You'll get your feathers back – but you'll be none the better for them!'

The goodwife walked home, fuming. When she found no feathers waiting for her there, she was crosser than ever. Her servants and milkmaids suffered the sharp edge of her tongue all the rest of the day. However, the cattle were giving out some of the finest, creamiest milk she'd ever tasted, so she was mollified a little. The maids set pail after pail by the door of the milking shed, until a good long line of them sat there.

Just as they were getting up and stretching their aching backs, one of the maids heard a noise. A small, soft noise, like a flurry of snow settling around her. She looked up, and there, in the sky above was a cloud full of goose feathers. She called out and the goodwife came running.

The goodwife ran to the dairy shed, and the feathers swarmed around her, nipping and stinging like bees as she tried to snatch them from the air. But she couldn't grab any of them. They sailed over her head, and one after the other, the feathers fell into the pails of frothy milk.

The feathers and the milk were ruined. The goodwife was furious. The maids whispered the tale around the town, and soon everyone was buzzing with it. More people lined up at Nan's door after this proof of her powers, but the goodwife went to the vicar and told him what had happened.

The vicar laughed long and loud. He said, 'I'd challenge God to come up with a more fitting punishment than that of old Nan Barrett!'

After that, there was no one in Eye who would not pay Nan her due.

East Anglian witches of both sexes were to suffer some of the worst persecution in the country during the seventeenth century. The Witchfinder General Matthew Hopkins caused the deaths of sixty-eight so-called witches in Suffolk alone. Most of these were vulnerable people with no families to care for them.

SIX

CAP' O' RUSHES

In Bury St Edmunds there lived a rich merchant whose wife had died long ago, leaving him with three small daughters. The merchant had loved his wife, and he vowed he would bring up his daughters well, in memory of her. But he was a merchant. The only way he knew to show love was to lavish the girls with gifts. Throughout their childhood, they were given the very best toys and the finest tutors that his money could buy. Now that they were young women, he brought home bolts of the softest silk and the richest velvet. They lacked for nothing, but the rich man couldn't help but notice that when he came home after a trading trip his daughters' eyes would first light on his bundles of gifts before they lit on him.

He realised that maybe all they loved about him were the gifts he brought home. So he decided to test his daughters and find out which one loved him the best. That one, he decided, would inherit all his riches, and the others, well; they would have to shift for themselves.

He called his daughters together and sat them down, and told them they were going to play a little game. To his eldest girl he said, 'Tell me how much you love me.'

The eldest daughter was surprised at the question. All her life, they'd basked in his love and attention. How could anyone doubt that she loved her daddy?

She said, 'Why, Daddy, I love you as much as I love my life!'

The rich man was pleased at that.

Then he turned to his second daughter and asked, 'How much do you love me?'

The second daughter was already ready with her answer.

'Daddy, I love you more than the whole world!'

The rich man was pleased at that, too.

Then he turned to his youngest girl, the one who was always the first to fling her arms around him when he returned. She was his secret treasure, even though it was because of her that his wife had been lost. What, though, could she say that would be better than the first two had said?

Having listened to her sisters, the youngest girl frowned; she knew how they spoke of their father when he was not around. When it came her turn to answer, she wracked her brains for something that would show the depth of her love.

'Daddy, I love you as much as meat loves salt.'

The rich man stared at his daughter. As much as meat loves salt? What did that mean? Anger rose up in him. Had he nurtured a viper in his nest all this time? She didn't love him at all.

'I see now how it is,' he said. 'I have two daughters who love me and one who does not. You will leave this house and go, and if I never see you again it will be too soon!'

The youngest girl couldn't believe her ears, but she was as proud as her father and if he didn't understand her then she wasn't going

to explain. She went to her room and packed a bag with her finest clothes – a merchant's daughter is always practical – and, without looking back, she left.

She ran until she was out of the town and heading north towards the fen country, with no thought in her mind but to get as far away as possible. She followed the River Lark as it meandered through the fields. The farmers stopped in their work to stare at the pretty young woman, but there was something in the way she stared straight ahead that stopped them from calling her over. She walked until she was away from anyone, and then she lay down in a copse and tried to sleep. It was a long night, but in the morning she arose without complaint and walked on.

She walked until she could walk no more. When she looked up she found herself in a rippling sea of reeds and rushes. She was too exhausted now to be angry, and she knew she couldn't just keep walking without a plan. She knew too that she was in danger, a young woman in fine clothes, alone and unprotected.

As she looked at the rushes, she had an idea. She took out her knife and started to cut them down. When she had an armful, she sat down and began to weave. After a long evening's work, she held up what she had made, smiled a grim smile and swung her handiwork over her shoulders so that she was entirely covered by a cape of rushes.

She set off walking again into the night. It wasn't so long before she saw lights in the darkness. A fine manor house rose out of the gloom; exactly what she needed.

She walked up to the servants' entrance and knocked on the door.

A large woman in a floury apron opened the door and took in the ragged figure.

'We don't need no Gypsies here,' she said.

'I can work. Do you need a maid?'

'We don't need anyone,' said the cook. 'Now be off with you!'

But when the girl dropped the hood of her cape, the cook melted at the sight of her great, sad eyes.

'Well, if you can wash dishes for just your bed and board, then we might have a place for you.'

It was only after she had installed the girl in front of the sink, and her mean bundle was deposited on a thin pallet by the hearth, that the cook realised that the girl had given no name.

So they called her 'Cap' o' Rushes', after the cape she never took off.

Cap' o' Rushes kept her head down. She didn't shirk the meanest jobs. It was a good place, with a kind master and a courteous mistress. The jewel of the place, though, was their son, a golden-haired young man. Cap' o' Rushes smiled to herself when she saw him, but she said nothing and bided her time.

After she had been there a few weeks, there was a great to-do. One of the neighbours out Cavenham way was to give three balls, and the young master was to attend, and the servants were allowed to walk over and watch. The maids, in great excitement, were full of talk of the great event. Cap' o' Rushes said nothing, until the maids begged her to come with them.

'Oh no,' she said. 'Not me. I'm so tired after all that washing up. Just tell me about it when you get back.'

But when the maids had gone, she grabbed her bag and went to the well. She washed off the grime of work, put on the fine clothes she'd taken from her father's house, and brushed out her hair so it shone like autumn leaves. Then she stowed her cape under her pallet and went out into the evening light.

When she arrived the ball was in full swing. She held her head high. As soon as she entered the room all eyes were on her. But she had just one aim in mind. She walked straight over to where the son of her house stood and curtseyed in front of him. And he, he thought he had never seen a woman more beautiful. Together they glided onto the dance-floor and there they stayed.

But before the dancing was over, and without saying a word, Cap' o' Rushes slipped out of his arms and out of the house. By the time the maids got home, she was wrapped in her cape and asleep on her pallet.

She smiled as she listened to the maids' excited chatter about the mystery girl.

'How I wish I'd seen that. Maybe tomorrow night.'

When the next night came, she protested she was too tired again. But when the maids had gone, Cap' o' Rushes was back in her finery and racing on her way to Cavenham. She was soon back in her young man's arms and dancing, dancing. But long before the dance ended she drew away from him. He tried to stop her.

'Don't go! At least, tell me your name.'

Cap' o' Rushes shook her head and smiled her sad smile and was gone.

When the maids came back, they talked again of the beautiful stranger and how the young master was besotted. Why, he hadn't danced with anyone after she had gone! They were sure he would propose to her by the end of tomorrow.

The next night Cap' o' Rushes once more waited for the maids to go, and then she was in her finery and off to Cavenham. Once more, she and the young master danced the night away, but when she was about to go, he caught her hand.

'Please don't go. Don't you know I love you? Tell me who you are and I will go to your father and ask for your hand.'

Cap' o' Rushes shook her head and tried to pull away.

The young master's eyes filled with sorrow, but he kept hold of her hand a moment longer and slipped a ring on to her finger.

'Take this as my token, and believe me when I say that if I don't see you again I shall die.'

When the maids came home they were full of the story. Cap' o' Rushes listened and smiled her sad smile.

News soon came to the servants' hall that the young master was searching the land for the beautiful stranger. Riders were sent to Bury, to Newmarket, to Cambridge and Thetford and all around, but there was no sign. The young master took to his bed and his parents were beside themselves with fear that he would die.

The mistress came down to the kitchen, wringing her hands, and instructed the cook to make soup to tempt her son. But the soup, like everything else, came back untouched, and the young man grew weaker and weaker.

Cap' o' Rushes watched this, and one day she came into the kitchen and found the cook in tears.

'The young master will not eat for all I do,' she sobbed.

'Let me try,' said Cap' o' Rushes.

The cook resisted at first, but she was so upset that in the end she let Cap' o' Rushes make the soup. At the last moment before it was taken up Cap' o' Rushes slipped the young master's ring into it. While the cook took up the soup, Cap' o' Rushes went quickly to the well and washed herself, then put on her fine clothes, slung her cape over the top, and waited.

The young master toyed with the soup, and eventually he took a sip. He nearly choked on something hard. He spat it out into his hand. He stared at it. His eyes did not deceive him. There was the ring he had given his beloved.

He called for the cook. 'Who made this soup?'

The cook was afraid and said she had made it.

The young master shook his head. 'That can't be true. Tell me the truth and you will have nothing to fear.'

So the cook told him that it was Cap' o' Rushes.

The girl was summoned. She ran up with light steps to the young master's room.

'Did you make this soup?' he asked.

'I did,' she said.

'And where did you get this ring?'

'From him that gave it me,' and with that she pulled off her cape and stood there in front of him in all her finery.

After that, the young master was soon well. A wedding was planned, but Cap' o' Rushes still didn't reveal her real name. All the best people from around and about were invited, and Cap' o' Rushes made sure her father's name was on the guest list.

The day before the wedding, she went down to the kitchen and told the cook, 'When you make the feast, make sure that you use no salt.'

'That will be right nasty,' said the cook.

'That doesn't matter,' said Cap' o' Rushes.

Just as the cook had thought, when the guests sat down to eat on the wedding day, they all exclaimed that the food had no taste.

Cap' o' Rushes' father burst into tears and cried out, 'What a fool I am. I had a daughter who told me that she loved me as meat loves salt, and I thought that she didn't love me at all and I threw her out. Now I see that without salt, meat is nothing. She loved me the best of all, and I have lost her. For all I know she might be dead.'

No sooner had he spoken than Cap' o' Rushes was at his side. 'Here I am, father,' she said.

And after that they all lived happily.

This is another story from the Fison sisters. Again, it was told by their West Suffolk servant. The Fison family was originally from Barningham, not far away from Bury and Cavenham. This story echoes two very familiar tales, Cinderella and King Lear. Salt was a vital ingredient in the past. It is difficult for us now, in our refrigerated, low-sodium world to reckon the importance of salt as a preservative and a flavour, but the number of tales that allude to it can give us an idea.

SEVEN

STOWMARKET FAIRIES

John Suttle of Onehouse was not a subtle man. He was given to long drinking sessions at the Shepherd and Dog, and he loved to gossip. But there was one secret he would never tell: the secret of his own prosperity. John had a cottage at the far end of the village of Onehouse on the road to Stowmarket, and he'd lived there all alone since he was eighteen and his old mother had died. At first he'd struggled, and the house was everything that you'd expect of a bachelor's pad – it was dirty, untidy and starting to crumble. But after a while he seemed to get a grip. The house was tidy now, and John had a job as a farm labourer. The elders in the village complimented the young man on how he had turned himself around. But his clean living wasn't the reason for his pristine house. No, that was the secret that John had sworn never to tell.

Once a month, John knew to make sure he was in the house and locked away in his bedchamber, because once a month the fairies made John's house their meeting place. It was a rowdy, noisy affair: music blaring, the lights burning more than half the night, and it sounded as if they were turning the place upside down. The first time it had happened John had cowered on his bed all night and ventured downstairs the next day with shaking legs, so fearful was he at what he'd find. But the house was spotless. It was such a shock to John, considering the mess he'd left it in the day before, that he sat down on the bottom step and stared.

As he stared, a figure emerged from the shadows and approached him. A tiny figure, no more than three foot tall, with sandy hair and skin, wearing the strangest clothes: a long green coat, yellow satin shoes and a golden belt.

'John Suttle,' the little man said, 'we'll be coming every month from now on, and we like a place to be neat and tidy, not like the pit you were living in. Once we week we'll come and clean, and we'll leave wood in the oven, and a shilling under your chair. But if you mention one word of us to anyone, we'll be gone as if we'd never been.'

Every week they came, and it was just as he'd said: the warning, the tidying and the shilling. And once a month, the rowdy meeting. John longed to tell the world that the ferishers did for him, but he steeled himself and kept silent for six long years, and put the shillings away and prospered.

By the time he was twenty-five, he began to think about how lonely the house was, and that it would be very fine to fill it with a family. There was a woman he fancied, Mary, the cousin of one of his fellow labourers, who lived out on the Bury road. Mary was a pretty girl, but what truly drew John was that she often told a tale of how once, when she was a young girl, she'd seen the ferishers in their spangly dresses dancing by the hop ground near where she lived.

Mary liked John well enough and was happy to consent to marry him. But when she saw how neat his house was, she laughed and said there would be nothing for her to do.

'It's so tidy even a ferisher would live here!' she cried.

John longed to tell her the truth, but he didn't dare. He did wonder, though, whether Mary would like actually sharing her house with the fairies. The closer the wedding got, the more it preyed on him, so on his wedding night, after he and Mary had proved that they were indeed one flesh, he told her.

The fairies never came back.

Mary never quite forgave John, or the fairies. Their disappearance left her with a mountain of housekeeping. The loss of the weekly shilling left them poor. Soon there wasn't enough money to keep up the old house, and John and Mary moved their growing family to Stowmarket, where John worked in the brickyard on Tavern Street and hoped that moving to the big town had banished any foolish thoughts of fairies from their lives.

But they found it was harder to get rid of talk of the fairies than they had hoped. The area around Stowmarket was infested with them, and they even dared the town itself. It was the Suttles' youngest daughter, Sara, who kept on about them. John and Mary knew it was their fault, as the story of the fairy meetings was told so many times in their house it was as if John was trying to make up for six years of keeping silent. Sara was fascinated, and thought it most unfair that both her parents had seen the fairies and she'd never caught a glimpse of even one.

Everyone said that the brickyard where her father worked was their favourite haunt. As a child Sara would hide there with her friends at night, and watch the wood-stack – just in case.

'Sometimes you'll see them dancing,' her friend would whisper. 'At midnight, they race up and down Tavern Street, stealing little things – a piece of cheese, a scrap of lace, a nip of brandy – and then they come here.'

'If we see them,' put in Sara, 'then everyone will know because we'll get sparks of fire under our feet as we walk along!'

'Shh,' said another friend. 'If we make any sound at all, we'll never see them.'

So they watched, and longed, but the fairies never appeared.

As Sara got older, she got more and more disgruntled that they'd never seen the fairies. One day, at the end of one of the watching sessions, she stamped her foot and declared, 'I'm not coming here again – it's for babies! And I don't believe in the ferishers at all – it's all just stories. My pa was having me on.'

It was only a few short years later that Sara married Tom Steggles, a tammy cloth weaver. Tom rented a house by the Vicarage gate, and Sara was overjoyed to have her own home at last, even if it was draughty and full of holes. She was delighted in her husband, and a year later she and Tom celebrated the birth of a fine son.

When Sara found herself pregnant a second time, she thought her happiness was complete. But this pregnancy was difficult, and when her new son was born he was ill and fretful from the first. Before he was six months old, he died, and Sara was plunged into grief. She knew that it was common – two of her sisters had lost a child, she herself had watched a brother die before he was one – but she discovered that losing her own baby was very different. She ran over all the things she should or shouldn't have done, and her mind eventually took her to her childish renouncement of the fairies, and she shivered.

When Sara got pregnant again, she rocked her lost son's empty cradle to secure the new child's health, and tried not to think about the fairies. She was brought to bed with a girl, who thrived from the first. But Sara was terrified that the child would be taken, and kept her with her all the time, day and night. Sometimes she would take the babe to bed with her and Tom, to soothe the child's cries. She loved to feel the sturdy, warm little body cuddled up against her own.

One night, she woke up knowing something was wrong. At first, she couldn't work out what it was. Then she realised that the child was gone. Frantically she searched the bed, terrified that she or Tom had rolled on the babe. But her daughter was nowhere to be found.

Then, there was a small noise from the floor. At once Sara knew what had happened. The fairies were taking their revenge for her disbelief. She scrambled over her still sleeping husband, and slid to the floor, drew the curtain slightly to let the moonlight in, and there, on the floor at the end of the bed, was her babe. For one chill moment she thought the child had fallen, but then she saw the little sandy-coloured figures that moved quickly around it. She watched,

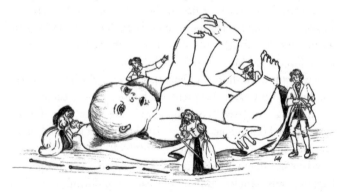

transfixed, as they gingerly pulled out the pins that secured the baby's napkin. Then, very slowly, she crept forward, hands outstretched to grab the child. But the old floorboards betrayed her with a creak.

Immediately, the fairies looked up. Shrieking, they fled through the cracks in the floor. For a long moment Sara listened as their laughter echoed under the floor, then she was across the floor, snatching up her baby, cuddling her close. The baby began to wail, and that woke Tom.

He was surprised to see his wife standing by the bed, cradling their daughter in her arms. Seeing him, she pointed at the floor, and murmured, 'The ferishers came…'

Tom looked down and gasped, for there were the pins laid out neatly, head to head and tip to tip in a line across the floor. Quickly, Sara told her tale, and Tom shook his head.

'They'd not want to take cold steel into fairyland,' he said. 'Them's not stupid.'

After that night, Sara was even more cautious, and pinned her small daughter not only into her bedclothes but also onto the bed itself. If she was glad to have seen the fairies at last, she never admitted it; just watched her daughter with even more care than before and was careful to praise the ferishers whenever they were mentioned.

Her daughter grew up healthy and strong – and just as fascinated by fairies as her mother had been. And maybe the fairies had blessed her after all, for Sara's daughter lived beyond her eightieth year. Right to the end of her life she believed in the fairies, and told the tale of her near-snatching to all who would listen. But then she would shake her head and wonder why it was that of late years no such things had been seen.

Stowmarket and its environs seem to have been absolutely infested with Suffolk's distinctive sandy-coloured fairies, known as 'ferishers' in the county. Revd Arthur Hollingsworth, vicar of Stowmarket and Stowupland in the mid nineteenth century, collected many tales of them in his History of Stowmarket *of 1844. But he wasn't the first to tell fairy tales of the area. 'The Green Children' and 'Malekin', both thirteenth-century tales, were also located near Stowmarket.*

EIGHT

THE BELLS
OF MINSMERE

There was once an old man and an old woman who lived on the
outskirts of the village of Eastbridge, on the edge of some of the
only remaining woodland in the parish. After hoping for many
years, they were blessed with two fine boys, just when they thought
time was running out.

The man's family had lived on that spot for many generations.

'We've bin here 500 year,' he would say. 'And now we've got our
boys, we'll be here 500 more!'

The house wasn't that old. It had been altered so much over the
years that little of the original house remained, but the couple had
something ancient that seemed to prove its age. Hanging over the
door as you came into the house was a small, grimy, earthenware
bell. It had no clapper, and looked like it had been mended many
times. The boys would ask what it was, but the old man and
woman would only say, 'That'll keep us safe here, you'll see!'

They were not rich, but they had enough. A plot of vegetables,
a cow for milk, a pig, and lots of chickens whose eggs they would
sell. They were happy even through the hard depression years, with
their two sons grown to young men and able to help on the farm.

Then the war came. First the older boy went off to fight, and
then the younger. The old couple had a couple of raw lads from the
city to help on the farm, but it was hard. And it would get harder.

Their boys didn't come home. First one telegram came, and then another. All their hopes were destroyed, but they had no choice but to soldier on.

'I'll not complain,' said the old man. 'We've had much joy, you and me.'

But his wife wished their joy could have gone on just a bit longer. If only her boys were back, getting settled and married and giving them grandchildren. She knew her husband wished that too. Who would not?

They tried to carry on as before. The city boys were gone home, but they had a lad to help them, and at first all seemed well. But by the beginning of the 1950s the two of them were into their seventies, and things became more difficult. Their bodies were just too old for heavy farm work, and so the farm started to get away from them. Someone said they might be entitled to one of these new state pensions, but there was no one to explain how it all worked and how to fill in the forms, so they just let it lie and tried to struggle on as they were.

As things worsened both of them began to look at the bell above the door, and wonder.

The story the old man never got around to telling their boys was this. Not all of the people of Eastbridge were originally from the Theberton area. Some of the villagers had arrived in the sixteenth century from Minsmere on the coast, and they had come carrying little earthenware bells.

In 1182 the landowner Ranulph de Glanville endowed a little abbey on the land looking out to sea. It was a lonely place, of marsh and dark forest and the ever-shifting sea, but ideal for the small community of monks to pursue the worship of God in isolation. The isolation didn't last that long. Because of the abbey, people were drawn to the area. A little settlement of fishermen grew up not far from the abbey, eking a living from the sea.

People said the place might boom, like Dunwich, but there was a problem. Sickness. It began with headaches and nausea, which rapidly spiralled into a terrible raging fever. Vomiting and diarrhoea followed. The victim's temperature would go up and up.

Many died, and those who didn't succumbed to the sickness again and again.

To the monks it was clear what was causing it. The marsh was infested with evil spirits that came in off the sea in terrible pea-souper fogs. They were sure too that the unhappy spirits of the dead who had died raving and cut off from God could only be adding to the evil that lurked out there in marsh and wood. So they prayed, and things did improve, but still people died. In 1363 the decision was taken to move the abbey inland to Leiston. The monks stripped the church of anything useful and left.

There was no escape for the villagers. They kept on dying, and with the churchmen gone, the haunting by the spirits got worse. A thick mist surrounded the village at all times, but there was always less mist at the ruins. At first the villagers ascribed it to a couple of hermits who lived in the ruins of the abbey. Eventually, even the hermits left. The nearest church was now the one at Theberton, and the priest there was not interested in this distant settlement away across the treacherous marsh.

Life went on despite the sickness and haunting. The villagers stripped stones from the abbey for their houses. One day, a man took a small brass bell that he found lying on the ground. He was proud of this bell, and hung it up over the door of his cottage for all to see.

The very next day he was lost at sea, and after that even the abbey was shrouded deep in mist.

It was clear to the villagers that the bell was to blame, and they took it back to the abbey and buried it with care. After that, the abbey was clear of mist again. The villagers realised that the bell was good luck, but only at the abbey. Eager to bring the magic to their homes, the villagers came up with another plan. They dug up the sandy earth from the abbey, mixed it with clay, and fashioned it all into little bells which they hung up by their doors.

The next time the fog rolled off the sea, the villagers heard a strange sound. It was as if there were church bells ringing all over the village. Sometimes, if the wind was right, they could hear Theberton's church bells, but this was different. The sound was coming from their homes. From the clay bells. The bells rang even though they had no clappers.

The fog caused less grief after that day, and fewer people died as the evil spirits were kept away.

But there was another enemy. The sea. By the sixteenth century the village was in danger of being washed away. The remaining villagers had to leave. They packed up their belongings and moved to Eastbridge. They took their bells with them and hung them up in their new homes to keep away the spirits, and the bells continued to work in this new place. Each generation passed the story down and warned their children never to remove the bells.

The old couple knew another tale of the bells as well. It was said in hushed tones that there were words and deeds to make the spirits help in one specific way if the need and the desire were there. As time passed, the old man and his wife said nothing, but both began to think about the release that the spirits could bring.

In 1954 the old woman became very sick. She recovered, but she couldn't do the work she had done before. With no money left to pay the lad, everything fell on the shoulders of the old man.

One day, the old woman called him to her at the end of the day.

'Now, you know and I know that we can't go on like this. What are we going to do about it?'

The old man's gaze slid over to the bell.

'That's it,' said his wife. 'You and I shall make a pact that we'll go out together – and die happy. You know what to do.'

The old man went to the door and took down the bell, and together they crushed it up until it lay in many little pieces. Then they took the bits and chucked them in the fire and watched until there was nothing left but dust. They hobbled out into the wood, scattered the dust and said the words they were sure would bring the spirits. That night they opened all the windows and the door, and then lay down together on the bed and wrapped their arms around each other as they had done every night of their married lives, and they waited.

At midnight there was a low moaning sound, and fog seeped into the house. The old couple didn't pay it any mind, just held tight to each other and waited. By dawn the mist was gone.

The next morning, by chance, the lad came to check on them. He found them still and stiff in their bed. He ran off to fetch someone, and when the villagers came they couldn't help but notice that the bell was gone.

No one would take on the place without that protection. The cottage was used as an animal shed, and soon fell into disrepair. By the 1970s it was a ruin, and in the 1980s it was pulled down. A new place was eventually built nearby, but it won't have a bell. The changes in the lives of villagers have been so great since the old couple died that such things are all but forgot.

Minsmere is now a wildlife reserve, but the ruins of the old abbey can still be found close to the sea, just behind the coastal defences. Stories of the bells were gathered by Robin Ellis and Jude Avery a few years ago, but if you ask in the Eel's Foot in Eastbridge now, sadly no one knows the tale.

NINE

FRIAR BUNGAY AND THE FAIR MAID OF FRESSINGFIELD

Thomas of Bungay was a bright boy; so bright that a few short years after going to Norwich to be a Franciscan friar, he was sent to the university at Oxford to study and teach. There, he caught the attention of another bright young man. Roger Bacon and Thomas Bungay were soon firm friends, because they shared a passion not only for philosophy and science, but also for the magical arts.

The thirteenth century was filled with war and, across the Channel, France was looking aggressive. The King, Henry III, was (whisper it) weak. Bungay and Bacon decided that Britain needed protecting. Their reading led them to believe that a wall of brass around Great Britain would be the answer. That would keep the enemies out! But how to do it? Only the help of a demon would do, so they called one up.

The demon said, 'Make a head of brass, then make your hottest potions and feed them to the head. In a month, or maybe less, the head will speak – but beware, if you both do not hear it, it will never speak again.'

For a month Bacon and Bungay fed the head. They didn't dare sleep, and became dizzy with tiredness.

At length Bacon said, 'We'd better sleep. My servant Miles can wake us if it speaks.'

Miles wasn't remotely interested in the magicians' work. He only listened with half an ear to Bacon's instructions. But when the brass jaw clicked open, he jumped to his feet to go and wake the snoring friars.

'TIME IS.'

The head said no more. Miles thought it best not to wake the friars for something so pathetic. After a while the jaw creaked again and the head spoke once more:

'TIME WAS.'

And again it was silent. Miles was uneasy, but before he could make up his mind the head spoke again:

'TIME HAS PASSED.'

And with that the head exploded in a spume of molten metal. Bacon and Bungay awoke into a chamber full of smoke with a pool of pinking brass on the floor. The experiment was over, and when the college authorities saw what a mess had been made of an expensive college room, they decided the friars should be separated from each other.

A professorship was hastily organised for Bungay at Cambridge, but before the separation took place, a letter came from the King summoning the friars to London. At first the friars were afraid that their trick had attracted royal anger, but in fact King Henry wanted them for a magical mission. They were to accompany him to Paris, where Louis IX was harbouring a German magician. They were to prove that England had stronger magic than France.

Louis presented the German magician, Vandermast. In front of all the court he conjured from the grave the semblance of Pompey as he was at the battle of Pharsalia. Bacon smiled, and conjured up the shade of Caesar, who had beaten Pompey. The two spirits leapt at each other, swords flashing in the sunlight, and soon Caesar was chasing Pompey back to hell and Bacon was smiling.

Vandermast was furious. He started towards Bacon, his hands raised, but Bungay was quicker. The Garden of the Hesperides sprang up in front of Vandermast. The courtyard was filled with the scent of apples and poppies; bees buzzed around the courtiers. In front of the garden was the great serpent Ladon, all 100 of his heads fixed on Vandermast and hissing.

Vandermast made a move, and suddenly Hercules strode out across the floor, his club raised, ready to snatch away the golden apples. But Bungay wasn't done; he made three passes with his hand and Hercules lowered his club, turned about, walked back to Vandermast, and picked him up. He carried him, kicking and screaming, straight out of the courtyard and away.

'I'll be back!' they heard him cry. 'Friar Bungay, I'll be watching you – one false move, and I'll have you.'

King Henry was delighted with the result, and he feted the sorcerers all the way back to London. But for Bacon and Bungay the journey home meant that they had to go their separate ways.

Bungay was soon at home in Cambridge. It wasn't that different from Oxford and there was plenty of open space to practice his illusions. He soon became well known for his fine teaching, and the sons of the rich flocked to his door to go out into the Fens with him and learn about natural science.

One such young man was Thomas de Lacy, the brother of the Earl of Lincoln. Lacy kept illustrious company. He was a great friend of Edward, Henry III's eldest son. After Lacy graduated, his friends joined him in East Anglia and they decided to go hunting at the royal castle at Framlingham. On the way, they heard that the Norfolk town of Harleston was having its annual fair, and so the young blades went there instead.

There, Edward fell in love with the most beautiful girl at the fair, Margaret, a gamekeeper's daughter from Fressingfield. Never mind that she was so lowly, never mind that Edward was already married; he had to have her. But to Edward and his friends she seemed protected by a gaggle of other girls. They couldn't get near her.

Edward declared as they rode away to Framlingham that he would put aside his wife for the 'Fair Maid of Fressingfield'. Maybe his friends weren't that loyal. Word reached King Henry, and to stop him doing anything rash, Edward was confined to the castle.

But Edward had plans. He selected a friend he knew was loyal: Thomas de Lacy.

'Go to Fressingfield and woo her in my name – and bring her back here for me.'

Lacy had no idea how to go about this, but he knew he couldn't disobey the Prince. And he had an idea about who might be able to help him. He rode back to Cambridge, and went straight to his old tutor's room. Bungay was surprised to see him, but welcomed Lacy in and listened to his problem.

'Fressingfield!' cried Bungay, with a twinkle in his eye. 'I do believe it will be their fair this week. But, my boy, if its magic you want, I would advise against it. Love and magic don't make good bedfellows. Just disguise yourself as a farmer so that she's not afraid, and I'm sure she won't be able to resist your wooing. If you have any problems, just let me know and I will come.'

Lacy went away relieved. By the time he arrived in Fressingfield he was disguised as 'Tom of Beccles', come to the fair to sell his wares and have a bit of fun. He soon spotted Margaret. She seemed lovelier than before. He realised with a sinking heart that Edward had set him a hard task, as Margaret was an easy girl to love.

Margaret was puzzled by this strangely well-spoken farmer, but he was handsome and he made her laugh. Soon she was in love, and she sensed that Tom loved her too. But there was something odd about him, nonetheless.

Lacy agonised. On the one hand, he was Edward's trusted friend. On the other, he loved Margaret. In truth he knew that Edward would never be allowed to marry her. The most she could expect was to be his mistress. Margaret didn't deserve that. Lacy loved her and knew she should have honour.

In the end, his honesty won, and he confessed all: his mission, and his own love. Margaret was horrified at first, but Lacy begged her to marry him.

'Imagine,' she thought. 'A gamekeeper's daughter as an aristocrat's wife!' She said yes, but then shook her head. 'No priest will marry us – we are too far apart in degree.'

Lacy smiled at that and remembered Bungay's promise.

'I think I know of one.'

Meanwhile, the King summoned Edward to Oxford. Edward was not in the mood for reconciliation, but Henry wanted to please him and took him to meet an old friend, Friar Bacon.

'You'll like it – he's a sorcerer. He once saved the honour of England, with his friend Bungay.'

Edward pricked up his ears at Bungay's name.

Bacon welcomed the King and Prince, and produced a small mirror.

'Name any person that you want to see, and they will appear in the mirror.'

Edward said, 'I want to see Margaret.'

'Absolutely not,' said King Henry.

'Very well,' said Bacon. 'I'll show you how it works. I've long wanted to see how my old friend Bungay is faring.'

He made three passes over the mirror, and there in the mirror was a man's face, talking away.

'No sound, I'm afraid,' said Bacon. 'I'm still working on it. Now that's a little too closely focused…'

He tilted the mirror. Bungay was revealed, talking to a young man and woman in a church. They were holding hands and looking solemn. Edward knew exactly who they were and was suddenly sure what was going on.

'Lacy, you betrayer!' He turned to Bacon. 'You have to do something! He's about to marry the woman I love!'

Back in Fressingfield, Bungay suddenly fell silent. He clutched his throat but no words came. Their wedding forgotten, Lacy and Margaret rushed to him, and tried to help. They took him back to his room in the village inn, and he grabbed a mirror and made three passes over it – and frowned at what he saw.

He quickly wrote something, and shoved it in Lacy's hand.

Lacy read, 'Bacon stopped my tongue. Prince Edward on his way.' Then he cried, 'We must hide!'

But Margaret wouldn't leave the village. Without a priest they couldn't marry, and all they could do was wait. They spent a tense night and day at her father's house until they heard the hooves of Edward's horse. Lacy went out to face him.

Edward drew his sword. 'Come and fight, you false friend! I'll have your head!'

Margaret came out and stepped in front of Lacy. 'Stop,' she cried. 'Your highness, please don't do this! He is your friend and I – I am a gamekeeper's daughter. What would the country say if I was to be queen? What would your wife say if she knew? I love Thomas and he loves me. Our union is scandal enough; we only beg your blessing.'

Edward's anger drained away, and he let his sword fall to the ground. He clasped their hands and gave his blessing.

Then they went to Friar Bungay, who was frowning at something he could see in his mirror.

'Is all resolved?' he asked. 'Bacon told me all and restored my voice. It gave me an idea. We've got round the sound problem, by writing notes. But he told me to beware – an old foe has spotted us through the mirror and he's on his way. So, we'd better be quick and proceed with this wedding. Will you stand witness alongside Margaret's father, your highness?'

None too soon, for once the wedding was done and the party walked onto the village green, the sky darkened into a swirl of clouds, and in the centre of the storm stood a man riding the clouds.

Bungay thrust the lovers and the Prince aside.

'Run!' he cried, then quickly drew a circle on the ground around himself.

Vandermast stepped out of the sky.

'For years I've waited for a glimpse of you! As soon as I saw you in Bacon's mirror, I knew that today was the day I would take my revenge.'

Vandermast raised a fiery dragon that scorched the edges of Bungay's circle with its flames; but Bungay was fast – he raised his arms and hauled the River Waveney down to Fressingfield so that it flooded the Green and a sea serpent rose out of it, snapping at the dragon.

Vandermast laughed, and raised Perseus against the serpent. Bungay raised St George against the dragon. The sea serpent was slain, and the river rushed back north, but throughout the village thatch was set alight as the dragon fled St George until at last there was a terrible reptilian screech and a fountain of fire rushed into the sky.

But Vandermast was not done. Quick as a flash he raised another spirit. The valiant Hector raced at Bungay, but Bungay raised Achilles and the two fought. They fought so hard that the

storm roiled around them, lightning flashed with their sword clashes, and thunder rang with their clanging shields. Around the clouds swirled, until a fog covered the whole of the Green. The villagers watched and waited, until with a final clap of thunder, the fog lifted and the sun shone once more.

Edward, Lacy and Margaret searched for Bungay, but neither he nor Vandermast was to be found, and it was a sad wedding party that set out to Oxford that day to tell Friar Bacon that he was now the only sorcerer in the land.

> Friar Thomas de Bungay was a real person, a member of the new Franciscan order. In 1270 he was a lector at Oxford, and soon became the head of the order in England. By the 1280s he was a lector at Cambridge. Whether he was ever a magician is a matter for debate, but he was certainly a friend of Roger Bacon and a scholar, who wrote on Aristotle's Physics. Some say he survived the battle and that he lived out his last years in a friary in Northampton writing a book on natural magic.

TEN

ST BOTOLPH AND THE DEVILS OF IKEN

Christianity was the new big thing in East Anglia, but there were as yet few places to study to be a priest. Botolph was lucky. He was rich enough to be shipped abroad by his proud parents to study at the esteemed Faremoutiers Abbey in France. Botolph learnt quickly and gained a reputation for compassion and knowledge. He made friends easily among the young nobles who came to study, but unbeknownst to him one friend, Saewara, a Kentish princess, would have a great effect on his life. When she married Anna, an East Anglian thane, he assumed he would never see her again, but fate was to prove him wrong.

East Anglia was a kingdom in turmoil. Gone were the safe days of Raedwald. King Penda of Mercia had his greedy eye on the kingdom. In 640 the monkish King Sigeberht fell in battle against Penda – not surprising, as he had gone into battle carrying only a staff. Word soon reached Botolph that Anna was King of the East Angles; his old friend Saewara was now a queen.

Anna was a good Christian, but he knew how to fight. Saewara worried that her children would grow up immersed in battle, and not in Christ.

She went to Anna and said, 'I know a good and holy man who would be a fine chaplain for you, and teach our children the ways of Christ.'

That man was, of course, Botolph. He arrived in time to baptise
Saewara's last child Wendreda in the holy well at Exning. He was
soon loved by all of Saewara's brood of girls and the one treasured
boy, Jurmin, and he earned the respect of Anna with his devotion
and wisdom.

But Saewara had been right to fear. Penda's eyes soon turned
back to East Anglia, and once more his force was the stronger.
Anna fled with his family to a kinsman in Shropshire and for three
long years they lived in exile. Anna chafed against it. Botolph
counselled patience. Without Botolph, Anna swore he would have
gone mad, and Botolph began to understand why God had called
him to this position.

In 654 Anna returned to Suffolk. He took his chaplain with
him, and his young son Jurmin, newly a warrior. But Penda was
waiting. For a year they battled back and forth across the land. In
early 655 Anna and Jurmin waited with their host at the edge of
the marshes in the Blyth estuary, close to their royal home and the
little monastery there.

'This will be the battle to end it all,' Anna swore.

So it proved, but not how Anna hoped. Penda's army was so
strong that Anna and Jurmin were pushed back into the woodland
close to the edge of the marshes. Anna urged his son to flee to the
river. Boats were waiting in case of need, to spirit him to the coast,
but even as the boy ran for the water the Mercians closed in on the
King and his son and cut them down.

No sooner had they fallen than a gush of water burst from out of
the earth and poured over them.

It was Botolph who found them. He fell down his knees at the
sight. All around was a carnage of mud and blood, but the bodies
of the King and Prince were washed clean, their wounds gone.
A miracle, but a dark one. His heart bleeding and full of despair,
Botolph saw the bodies back to the monastery at Blythburgh.
He oversaw their burial. He declared the still-flowing spring to be
a holy well, open to all travellers.

His duty done, he went to the new kings of East Anglia,
Athelwold and Athelhere, and begged a lonely place to start a

monastery in honour of his fallen king and prince. A place, though he didn't say it, where his soul might heal, away from the world of battles and politics.

The new kings were only too happy to grant his request.

'There is a place where cattle graze by the Alde,' said Athelwold.

'A lonely, quiet place,' said Athelhere. 'If you can defeat the devils that live there.'

Botolph smiled. 'It will be my pleasure.'

It was a nervous group of monks that made their way down to Iken, and their unease grew when they arrived to discover water lapping at their toes, and a boat.

'It's only an island at high tide,' said the farmer who accompanied them. 'I'll row you over now, but you'll have to wait until low tide to walk out. Mind you watch out for them devils, now.'

As soon as Botolph landed he fell to his knees in grateful prayer, but the other monks watched the boat go with rising horror. From a small cliff rising up back toward the old cemetery at Snape, there extended an expanse of reed-beds. All was marshland. And they were alone in it.

Suddenly a noise rose from the marshes as if something large was breathing heavily nearby, and the monks started in terror.

Once on the island, Botolph led them in a service of thankfulness, but few of the monks felt thankful. With night came the

sound of owls hooting, and the rustling of small creatures nearby. Many of the monks lay awake that night. The next day, they went through the motions of laying out their new church and housing, but as they worked they heard that heavy breathing and a whistling, shrieking sound. To make it worse, by nightfall a terrible smell had settled over the island.

One of the monks made a run for it, racing along the sandy beach under the cliff, but he hadn't realised how fast the tide came in. The others could only watch as he was swept away.

Botolph led them in prayer. Then he told them, 'Remember that the fathers of the church fought demons in the wilderness – and won, to the glory of their souls. If we pull together, and trust in Jesus, no demon can harm us.'

Their souls eased slightly, the men settled to sleep. But the next morning they found that the foundations of the church had been dismantled and scattered across the island. Doggedly, they gathered them up and started again. But each day it was the same. Their buildings were torn down in the night, the day was haunted by strange sounds from the marshes, and the awful smell lingered.

After a week, Botolph decided that it had gone on long enough. 'We will recite the prayers of exorcism, and we will not stop – not to sleep, not to eat – until the demons are gone. We will show them we are strong and we will never give in!'

He erected wooden crosses at all corners of the island, and then for three days and three nights they prayed.

At the end of the third night, a great shrieking and wailing rose from the marshes. The monks scrambled up. They swore they saw something large and dark sliding away through the reeds; banished, it seemed, by their prayers.

After that, Iken became a place of peace and joy. The church was built, and more monks came to live there. Holy men visited to observe Botolph's calm and gentle rule. Botolph went away to found churches in Kent and elsewhere in East Anglia, but he always returned to his peaceful island. He died on 17 June 680, twenty five years after founding the monastery. He was buried with great reverence on the island, and the monastery continued his good work.

For nearly two centuries Iken was one of the holiest places in Suffolk, but in the 860s the Vikings came. Ivar the Boneless and his men wreaked havoc all along the coast. Iken, where King Edmund had studied, was singled out for exceptional damage. The wooden church was smashed, the monks killed and the riches of the monastery taken. In the bleak years that followed no one came back to rebuild the church. But Botolph slept there still.

He was too holy a saint to be left alone in the marshes. In 970 the Bishop of Winchester demanded Botolph's bones be rescued, and sent a monk, Ulfkittel, to fetch them. When Ulfkittel arrived and uncovered the bones, he and his team found them so heavy they could hardly lift them. After many long hours they managed to extract the bones, and in respect Ulfkittel placed a grave marker on the spot to let everyone know Iken had once been a saint's home.

After hours of carrying the heavy bones on their backs, the monks ground to a halt at Burgh. The priest there was delighted to see them.

'We are infested with demons! St Botolph will chase them off if you'll leave him here.'

The priest explained that St Felix had buried gold on Whitefoot Lane between Burgh and Clopton. The saint had left a monk and a dog there to guard it. But after a few years the monk and the dog were both gone, and in their places was … something else. A galleytrot. A huge dog with a monk's head prowled the land, and everyone was terrified.

Ulfkittel didn't want to leave the relics, but the bones couldn't be budged from the church. For several years Burgh's ghost was quiet. But in 1020 King Cnut gave out a decree that the saint must go to Bury to join Suffolk's great hero, St Edmund. The monks were nervous when they came to take him away, remembering Ulfkittel's labours. They arrived in the black of the night, and there was no light in the church, but as they entered they saw that a light shone from the feretory where the saint was kept, and when they lifted the reliquary it was quite light, as if it rejoiced to be going to Bury.

Botolph's remains were eventually given to several monasteries, his power was considered so great. Back in Burgh, though, the galleytrot rejoiced that Botolph was gone. It crept out from where it had hidden, and it haunts Whitefoot Lane until this very day, guarding St Felix's treasure at Clopton Hall.

Iken is the most likely identity of Icanho, the name given as the location of Botolph's monastery. It still seems the ideal spot for a lonely monastery. There's a causeway now, but it's still easy to get cut off by the sea on the beach below the cliff. Maybe the demons were imagined from the water birds' cries, maybe they were disgruntled Iceni, the Celtic tribe that lived in this region, as Norman Scarfe suggests – or maybe they really were demons!

ELEVEN

THE RAT PIPERS
OF BECCLES

Midsummer 1349, and Beccles was in turmoil. The Black Death had
come dancing up the Waveney and now people were dying. There
wasn't a house in the town that wasn't affected, and the townsfolk knew
there was no escape as the towns and villages all around fell foul of the
plague. There was madness in the air as some gave in to the tempta-
tions of the flesh, and others tried to mortify it before it was too late.

With the Death had come another plague. The town was overflow-
ing with rats. There were always a lot of rats in Beccles, surging off the
boats, up the hill and into the houses, but this year, as the people grew
fewer, the number of rats increased. It was true that there were plenty
of dead rats everywhere, but more rats soon came to take their place. It
seemed as if Beccles was living on a seething carpet of rats.

Poison was set for the rats. Ratcatchers and their dogs were
brought in. People killed the rats whenever they saw them. But it
did no good. The rats kept coming.

On the 29 August, three men from very different walks of life sat
together in the Bear and Bells on the marketplace and declared they
couldn't stand it any longer. They were Peter Harris, Jonathan Bido
and Samuel Partridge. Each of them had lost his entire family in the
plague, with only themselves spared. This had created an unlikely
bond between a goldsmith, a tallow chandler and a pedlar. By the end
of the night they had a plan, and with set faces they went on their way.

The next morning they were seen heading across the market to St Peter's to pray for the removal of the rats. By noon they were in St Michael's praying for the same, and soon after in the chapel of St Mary's at the Lazar House. People began to whisper that they were touched by God.

By the end of the afternoon the three were at the Portreeve's office. The Portreeve looked the three men up and down: well-dressed Harris, roughly dressed Bido and ragged Partridge.

'What do you want?'

'We've found a way to clear the town of the rats,' said Harris.

The Portreeve was sceptical, but in these dark times he welcomed any possibility.

'If you can do that, then you will be heroes indeed,' he said, but when he asked how they would do it, the men held their tongues.

'It is for the town elders to decide,' said the Portreeve. 'Come back this evening.'

The Portreeve called the council together and told them what the men had said. 'And they only want payment when it's done.'

The council agreed that there was no risk, and a sum of 45,000 marks was agreed as payment. It was a huge sum, but everyone agreed that if by some miracle the rats were gone, it would be worth it.

The Portreeve returned to find the three men waiting for him. He told them about the vast sum offered.

'But', he said, 'it's only payable if there isn't a single rat left in the town by the end of tomorrow evening. If you manage it, I'll be waiting here with the money.'

The men agreed without a word of dissent.

The word ran through the town that the men were going to rid the place of the rats, and the people whispered about how God must smile on the men, survivors as they were.

But the men's plan had nothing to do with God.

That night, under cover of the evening mist, they made their way along the river bank, past the bridge, the wharfs and the silent boats, until they were out in the reedy country beyond. The reeds stretched on into the moonlit distance, unbroken save for the rickety roof and smoking chimney of a hut. A hut where witches were said to live.

The three old women who lived in the marshes hadn't been seen in the town since the Death began, but everyone knew they were there. Sally, Nancy and Fanny were well known. A year or so before the Portreeve had tried to move them on, and for a month afterwards the puddings of the town were infested with flies. Our three men with a mission reasoned that if these women could bring flies, they could take away rats.

Partridge knocked on the door.

Immediately a voice cried out, 'Away with you plaguy men!'

'Not us, Nancy,' called Partridge. 'We had it and survived – it'll not catch us.'

The door creaked open, and an old woman's face stared out.

'What do you want, pedlar?'

And Partridge explained how they needed to get rid of the rats.

The old woman laughed at that, but she invited the three in. Inside it was dark and smelt of sharp herbs and … other things. Two more women sat by the fire, stirring a big, black cauldron.

'We can get rid of them rats,' said Nancy. 'But there's a price.'

'We'll give you a mark each from our prize money,' said Harris.

Nancy gave him a long look, then nodded. 'And for that generosity you will be well rewarded. But that's not the price I meant.'

'It's your souls we're after,' said Sally.

'The Devil takes his due for his good deeds,' said Fanny.

The three men had been expecting something of the sort. God had done nothing save take all those they loved. They were prepared to give the Devil his due.

That night, the three men swore away their souls in a dark ceremony and were sent away clutching a small reed pipe each.

Word had got around, and a crowd gathered in the marketplace. At noon the men arrived, clutching their pipes in their hands, and there was a murmuring in the crowd. Everyone watched with bated breath as the men put the pipes to their lips and began to play. A mournful, haunting melody emerged, one that spoke of all the losses in the town and the suffering of those yet living. For a good five minutes they played.

Then rats began to appear.

Out from the houses they came, out from the churchyard and the open graves, up along the streets from the town. Rustling, chittering, squeaking and flicking their tails they came. People began to scream, but the rats were everywhere. Thousands of them, it seemed. They all stopped in front of the pipers, quivering with concentration.

Then the pipers' tune changed, and they turned and walked away towards the Score. A dancing gig filled the air, and the townsfolk felt their legs twitching, but that was nothing on the reaction of the rats. They raced after the pipers, scrabbling and scrambling over each other in their eagerness to follow them. They filled the street, and on they ran, down to the Great Bridge. They swarmed over each other in their keenness to get across the river, and the pipers led them on.

The townsfolk followed the rats down the hill, but they didn't dare cross the bridge. A few ran onto it and watched the pipers moving away into the marshes, the tune still ringing in their ears long after the pipers and the rats were out of sight.

Then they heard a splash. And another and another – until the air was filled with spray and the shrieking of rats. Someone pointed upriver. The water was boiling with rats. Everyone crowded onto the bridge to watch until the last rat was gone and the water was still.

The townsfolk went back to the town and searched their houses, but not a single live rat was to be found anywhere in Beccles. There was a festive mood as the town elders marched through the town carrying the money to the Guildhall. The Portreeve received it with due ceremony, then he went up the stairs, set the three bags of 15,000 marks down on the table and waited.

And waited.

The pipers didn't come. The Portreeve waited until he was dozing on the table, but even by midnight there was no sign. He waited until the end of a third day, but no men came. Eventually the money was put away and the men assumed lost in their heroic act.

Although the rats were gone, the plague still raged and people soon forgot about the pipers. Soon enough, as the Death took life after life, there were few left to remember. But by the end of the year the plague had eased, and by the next summer the people of Beccles were rebuilding their lives. Trade started again, and once more boats plied the River Waveney from the sea.

The night of 31 August 1350 was a clear one. Late that evening, a boat came up towards the port from Lowestoft. All the men on board were thinking about was getting into the Bear and Bells before dark. But then someone noticed a strange sound out on the marshes to the Norfolk side.

'There's someone out there playing pipes,' he said. 'Sad little tune.'

As they listened, it seemed as if the playing switched to the Suffolk side, and they saw a little shack with a rickety roof and a smoking chimney. The tune, so sad, so mournful followed them all the way upriver to the Great Bridge, first on one side of the river then the other. The men were thoroughly unsettled by the time they reached the wharfs. They told the men there what they'd heard – and were surprised when the men immediately went white and crossed themselves.

'The pipers! They're haunting the marshes!'

There was no sign or sound of them the next night, but the next year on the 31 August it was the same, and the year after, and so it has been every year from then until now – if you listen hard enough.

This story first appears in Charles Sampson's Ghosts of the Broads, *published in 1931. He gives it a long pedigree, saying that there are medieval records and a ballad. The references are thought to be a hoax, and the story bears a striking resemblance to the 'Pied Piper of Hamelin', but who's to say that that the pipers weren't an existing tradition in the town?*

TWELVE

THE ORWELL MERMAID

John Poling was a fisherman who lived at Pin Mill on the banks of the River Orwell. Every day he'd go out on the boats to bring back the herring. He was used to the rough seas, the stink of the fish and the terrible hours and pay. But he was restless. The smart Thames barges taking the farm produce down to London from the wharf at Pin Mill seemed to offer a better kind of life; a chance to see the sights and live a little in the capital. Every day he went down to the barges and asked if there was an opportunity, but until one came up he was stuck with the fishing. Out on the boats he'd spend as much time as he could away from his crew mates, gazing out at the grey North Sea and dreaming of a new life.

It was thanks to this habit of moping that she saw him. She'd never paid much attention to the boats before. She knew what they were, of course; all her kind did. She knew what the boats did – how they took the fish away and put nothing back. There was many a hungry belly under the sea caused by the landmen's fishing. She knew too that she should never go near those boats.

It was a sunny day and she wasn't thinking of anything much as she slid along under the water, feeling the sun on her back. Without a thought she jumped up out of the water to taste the air and there, right in front of her, was a boat. The man on it was staring right back at her.

She shot back under the waves and huddled there for a moment. But she was curious, and so she raised her head out of the water again. The boat was a little further off now, but the man was still staring at the sea. She realised that he couldn't have seen her. Otherwise he'd be doing something. She'd always been told that humans got excited when they saw her people. She watched as the boat drew away and wondered what he was staring at.

She thought about him all night long, and the next day she quickly swam to the place and waited. The boat soon came into view, and there he was again, staring in a dream. It was a darker day and so she dared inch a little closer. Finally she could see him properly. And he was beautiful. Golden-haired and blue-eyed. Not like the hairy men who lived beneath the waves. Not only that, but as he stood there he started to sing. It was a slow mournful song that she didn't fully understand, but it tugged at her heart, and she yearned for him.

The next day, and every day after, she was there, watching him and listening. She kept low in the waves so that the fishermen never saw her, but she followed the boat nonetheless. When the boat came to the mouth of the Orwell, she stopped. She'd always been told never to go to the land, but she watched the boat as it slipped away up the river and she longed to follow.

Her dreams were filled with him. She longed for him to notice her. If he did, she'd open her arms and then he'd jump – and she didn't dare think what would happen after that, even in the inky blackness of the night. If she could just see where he went, maybe she'd be happy.

So the next day she steeled herself, and when the boat returned to the Orwell she swam on up the river after it. The river water felt strange to her. Cold it was, and heavy, and clogged with strange plants. It smelt, and she could feel its griminess on her skin. But still she swam, marvelling at the wooded banks, the houses and the reed-beds.

At last, the boat pulled in towards a settlement. It was just a scatter of houses along the bank, with boats lined up half in and half out of the water. For a moment she hesitated – then, as the boat eased in among the others, she swam towards the shore. But the noise made her shy back. Men's voices, harsh and loud, women shouting, children screaming, dogs barking and machinery she didn't understand clanking and whirring.

She darted back into the deeper part of the river and tried to compose herself. When she came back near the boats, her young man had gone. She searched the faces on the bank, but he wasn't there, and she didn't dare show herself. She spent the night huddled up against the boat.

John hadn't gone far, just ducked into the Butt and Oyster with his mates. He too was unsettled, and as soon as they were sat down he said, 'There's something strange going on out there. Have you noticed it? I feel like there's something watching me.'

His mates just laughed and told him he was dreaming. 'There's nothing out there, bor, but fish and sea.'

After a pint or two, John put the feeling out of his mind and laughed along with his friends.

The next day he got the impression his words had taken root in his mates' minds. Everyone was uneasy as they set out down the river. There was something in the water. They glimpsed a dark shape under the still surface in the early morning light, and before they reached the sea, John was sure he had seen the flash of a huge fishtail.

After that it was the same every day. A flash of tail, the dark shape, the sense of a presence near them. Once John thought he glimpsed a pale face above the water by the woodland on the river-bank. Back on shore, his friends shunned his company as if he was suddenly bad luck. And perhaps he was.

Then one day, as they were nearing the sea, something made him turn and there she was in the water beside the boat. The most beautiful woman he'd ever seen was smiling up at him from the water, her white arms outstretched to him. For a moment, he felt compelled to leap over the rail into the water. Just in time, he managed to stop himself. Then the fear came. He knew what she was. He'd heard the tales ever since he was a little old boy. His mother, who'd come from Rendlesham way, had told tales of the mermaid who lived in a pond there.

'That would crome you into the water with that's sharp nails, that would.'

But she was so lovely. They stared at each other. She swam closer and smiled at him. Smiled a smile full of pointed, sharp teeth. John started back, turned and bolted for the boat's cabin. For a long moment, he stood panting in horror, but then he shook his head at his foolishness. He went back to where he'd seen her, but the mermaid was gone.

She knew she should feel elated. He'd seen her at last, and she'd seen something in his eyes that made her think he thought her lovely. But he'd just stood there, and then he'd run away. Maybe he didn't like her after all. Maybe she was a fool.

For a few days she swam about back in the sea, glorying in its salty clean wonderfulness. But she missed him, so when she saw the boat one day, she followed it. But he wasn't on the boat. She swam around and around it, but he wasn't there. So she followed the boat back to Pin Mill, crept into the harbour and waited.

Each day was the same; the long waiting and the disappointment that he was never there. But still she stayed, hoping against hope that he would come.

Then, as she waited, she overheard two men from his boat talking.

'It's a shame about that John Poling,' one said. 'I know he was never that keen, but to see him go like that! Back to the land, after that strange business.'

'Must've been his mother's blood,' said the other. 'Or maybe he thought there'd be more money working his grandfather's farm. We'll not see him here again, I reckon.'

When she heard that, the mermaid knew he was truly gone. He had thought her so hideous that he'd fled the sea and even the river, and hidden somewhere on land where she couldn't go. But although she'd lost him, she couldn't bear to go back to sea. So she stayed, hanging around the landing stage at dusk and dawn and swimming up and down by the wood, not caring if she was seen or not.

The seasons moved on, and with winter came heavy snow. One day, two men were walking down through the steep wood with their dogs to the pub, crunching and sliding through the snow. The dogs raced ahead, and after a minute, the men heard barking. They crashed down the slope as fast as they could and ran to the edge of the water. The dogs were going wild. When they pulled them away they saw a sight that would haunt them for the rest of their lives.

A woman lay dead in the snow at the water's edge, ice-white with long, straggly, greenish hair. But she was only a woman to the waist. From there she had a long fish's tail. They didn't know what to do, or what to make of it, so they pushed her back into the water and hightailed it to the pub.

They said nothing of what they had seen, but the rumour that there was a mermaid out there wouldn't go away. A shadowy shape moved in the water by the boats on dark nights. Men would hear a voice singing in the wood, high and clear in dawn mist, singing the old songs that even the old men had forgotten; songs of love and longing. And sometimes a fisherman would see a pale face above the water close up by the woodland bank, and think that maybe he had seen the ghost of a mermaid.

This mermaid is one of the traditional maids of the sea, but Suffolk is more famous for its freshwater mermaids, like the one at Rendlesham. These creatures were childhood bogeys possibly created to stop children straying too close to dangerous waters.

THIRTEEN

THE SUFFOLK BLACK
AND THE ESSEX RED

English dragons have long been territorial beasts, and each county has developed its own particular variety with its own peculiarities. But as the centuries have progressed, and humans occupied every corner of the land, fewer and fewer of their kind have been seen.

The Suffolk Black remained. Coal black from her head to the tip of her tail; spines up her back culminating in a tuft of them on her head. She spent much of her time prowling the southern border of her county, along the River Stour. There had been little activity to the north and west for a long time, but she still saw the Essex Red cruising along the river. She had to make sure her lands were safe. But that year, 1405, had not been a good one. A harsh winter and a wet spring had left the animals thin and few. The dragon far preferred her game wild, but there seemed to be less deer and more farmland every year.

She was hungry.

Human places were dangerous. Humans didn't like wild beasts. The wolf was gone, and the bear. She remained because she was canny.

But, oh, she was hungry.

So she left her lair on Kedington Hill at Little Cornard. East Anglian dragons had learned to burrow – no handy caves for them – and the ground above the lair, a field entrance, had the tell-tale sign of scorched and cracked earth. She crept along the field

boundary and down through the woodland where the oaks and ash
would shelter her until she reached the safety of the willows along
the river. There she slipped into the water and swam upriver.

Sudbury drew her. Even that far downriver she could smell the
intoxicating stink of a human town, and she dreamed of roasted
pig and plump children. Dangerous, yes. But, oh, so tempting.

The first to see her was a child tending sheep on the flood plain.
He fled back home, screaming he'd seen a great black dragon.
His mother gave him a clip around the ear and told him to stop
bothering her with his tales.

The next to see her was a woman doing her laundry at the river
by Middleton, on the Essex side. She screamed and dropped her
linen and ran back to the village. She tried to raise the alarm, but
when she said it was the Suffolk Black she'd seen, everyone laughed
and told her she was safe in Essex.

The alarm was raised at last by a Dominican friar out fishing on
the edge of Sudbury. Panic hit the town. Mothers scooped up their
children and fled indoors. Shutters banged shut. Bolts slid home.
People fled to the north of the town and begged their relatives and
friends for shelter. And a group of men armed themselves with
bows and arrows and headed down to the river.

The Black lifted her wings and shook off the water, then up she flew. The stink of humans all around her confused her senses, and she was nearly hit by the first arrow that zinged past. She let out a bellow of rage and took in the ranks of men ready to shoot her down. She didn't wait for more, but turned tail and soared off back to the south.

Past her lair she flew, angry and still hungry, following the river, not caring if the humans saw her. When she came to Bures St Mary, she saw St Edmund's Hill rising up south of the village – and there was a flock of fat, juicy sheep. She couldn't resist. With a kick to gain height, she caught the wind, then folded her wings in and plunged down to grab one in her long talons.

The sheep was so good that she had to have another. Then she spotted that the sheep were not alone. The shepherd was raising something in his hands – another bow? She didn't think, just swept down again, and the shepherd lay dead on the ground, his sling and stone fallen by his side.

After that the dragon went a little mad and the hill became a chaos of swooping talons and saw-like teeth and bleating sheep and blood. But the villagers had seen the carnage. A posse was got together. A runner was sent to Smallbridge Hall to beg Sir Richard de Waldegrave for help.

His archers and the villagers approached the hill with caution, watching the dark shape swooping over the summit. From the cover of the clay pits at the bottom, the archers loosed their first volley. They watched in horror as the arrows simply bounced off the dragon's skin with a ringing sound as if they'd struck armour.

The Black was angry. She spotted the cowering humans, and she let out a belch of fire to show her displeasure. The smell of roasting mutton filled the air. But the archers let fly another volley. It was too dangerous, and so she fled again. It wasn't safe to go straight to the Stour. She flew southeast to try to make her way back to the river and its wooded safety.

That route took her straight over Smallbridge Hall. Out poured more humans, more bows and more arrows. Even old Sir Richard, seventy if he was a day, waved his sword. It was too much.

There were even people on the riverbank. She had to get away. Anywhere. So she flew south again.

Over the river.

Over the border.

As soon as she was safe from the humans she realised her mistake. She plunged down as fast as she could into a pond in a wood just into Essex in the hope it would obliterate her scent.

Meanwhile, the archers and the villagers went back to St Edmund's Hill and gently carried away the shepherd and laid him in the church for burial. They carried away the burnt sheep as well, and that night there was a great feast of roast mutton at the Eight Bells in honour of the brave shepherd and the bold dragon.

Dragons live longer than we do; their lives run at a slower pace. In 1449 when the spotted Essex Red came back to patrol his northern territory. he immediately knew there had been an incursion. He sniffed around until he came to that pond close to the river on Wormingford land, and he knew. He could smell her. *She* had been there. He'd been waiting for this for so, so long. He rose up into the air with a bellow of challenge.

The first the Suffolk Black knew was a rumbling and shaking in the ground. She snorted flames in response, and the earth cracked and scorched once more. She crept out of her lair, and there, soaring over the woods and Middleton church tower, was the Essex Red. He roared a challenge. Her blood grew hot, and she bucked up into the air and roared back. This was no time for caution and skulking. She raced down to the river and then up Ballingdon Hill to charge the Red over the willow woods.

The Red was waiting for her. They shot back across the valley, racing and tumbling over each other all the way up Kedington Hill. They zoomed south, snapping and ducking, belching fire as they went. A farmhouse went up in flames, for ever after known as Burnt House Farm. Then they fell back to course over the water meadows by Henny Street. The grazing cattle fled. The word got around that the dragons were back.

People rushed down to the river. From Sudbury and Little Cornard on the Suffolk side they came; from Middleton and Henny Street in Essex. Whenever the Black was on top, the Suffolk folk cheered, and when it was the Red a roar came from the Essex side.

At length it seemed the Black was backing down. She bowed her head to the Red and rolled to show her belly. The Suffolk crowd booed and screamed and egged her on, but the Red crowed and danced above her. Then up shot the Black, and as everyone watched, the two wheeled around and around each other, almost touching, until they were so high that they were just dark specks in the sky. The clouds swallowed them and they were gone.

Dragons have never been seen in Suffolk since that day, 26 September 1449, but there have been many sightings in Essex. And it's strange, because people don't talk just of spotted red beasts there any longer. These days, dragons in Essex are both red and black.

These two incidents are recorded as fact: the 1405 incident by the monk John de Trokelowe, and the 1449 is in a book in Canterbury Cathedral's library. People are as proud today of the Suffolk Black as they were in the fifteenth century: a dragon was painted onto a field not far from Smallbridge Hall by a descendant of Sir Richard de Waldegrave to celebrate Queen Elizabeth II's Diamond Jubilee in 2012.

FOURTEEN

GUARDIAN OF THE BRECKLAND

The story of the Breckland has been a journey from primeval pine forest to serried ranks of Corsican Pine. In between, it was a place of rabbit warrens and heather, of poor soil and blowing sand. When farming was new in this country, people cut down the trees to make space to grow their crops and graze their animals. They mined the flint for their tools. Then came the rabbits, burrowing into the ground and chewing the grass down to the quick. The soil couldn't cope, and the sand took over. When the wind whipped across from the Fens, the sand would whirl across the Brecks like a dancer. And sometimes, you could hear a melody in the wind. The sound was like a raw wooden flute, whistling hollow round the bushes, mournful and haunting. Sometimes, it was said, you could see the flute player in his long brown coat standing in the eye of the storm.

The modern age came to the Brecks early. Its open spaces and dry soil made it ideal for the coming thing: aeroplanes. In 1934 the RAF opened an airfield at Mildenhall. It was bare and flat and empty, save for a small clump of pines at Mum's Wood. Bombing raids from Mildenhall started on the first day of the war, 3 September 1939, and continued without ceasing as the war dragged on.

Every night was the same for 149 squadron. Their destination would come in from Bomber Command. There would be a briefing, crews were assigned duties, and then, as darkness fell, out the planes would go.

'B for Bertie calling Flightpath. May we taxi on and take off? Over.'

'Hello, B for Bertie. Path answering. Yes, you may taxi and take off. Over.'

The propellers of their Wellingtons and Stirlings would spin, and off they went, swallowed by the clouds, flying into darkness while the men at the base waited for their return. Usually the wireless would alert the base to the planes' homecoming long before the planes came. But the ground crew were alert for the first low whine and rhythmic chunter of a heavy bomber returning. Alert too, for the sounds of German planes approaching to bomb them in return.

That night in 1940 was perfectly clear. The open sky above the airfield was spangled with a thousand stars. A full moon beamed down on the low, camouflaged buildings of the base. The wind had stilled, and all was silent.

In the wireless room a message came through: 'Bandits sighted, coming up fast from the coast, following the river. The Huns are making for the base, chaps!'

Immediately the base mobilised. Pilots tumbled from their beds and scrambled for their flying kit. Planes were rolled out of hangers. Gunners raced through the darkness to the gun emplacements. Guns were swivelled to face the sky. Aircrews asked permission to take off. The first plane taxied onto the runway.

Then the unmistakable sound of Junkers 88 planes were heard approaching.

The first shiver of a breeze rustled the pines in Mum's Wood.

Suddenly, a figure appeared in the middle of the runway. A man, dressed in a long flapping coat.

The exiting plane ground to a halt.

'Who's there? Declare yourself!' called a member of its ground crew.

The figure just stood there.

Now the breeze was really getting up. The wind sock snapped. The rope on the flag pole jangled. As the pilots and ground crew watched, the man raised something in his hands, and several men threw themselves on the ground in case it was a gun. Instead the haunting notes of a flute were heard across the base, soft and caressing.

Around the figure's feet the dry sand began to eddy and whirl.

Suddenly, the wind was roaring across the airfield. Nothing to check it, save the low buildings. The planes rattled and juddered as the panelling was torn from their wings. No chance of taking off now. A huge strip of corrugated iron was ripped from the roof of the mess. There was sand was everywhere – blowing, scouring, enveloping everything in its path. Mouths and eyes and hair filled with sand. Cockpits were clogged with it. You couldn't see your hand in front of your face.

The wind was so strong that the storm soon moved away from the base.

Up in the air, the battalion of German planes registered something coming.

'Sandsturm voraus – auf gleicher Höhe! Kommt mit großer Geschwindigkeit direkt auf uns zu. Abdrehen! Abdrehen!

As quick as they could, the planes soared high, turned and fled. The storm was always behind them. Whichever course they took, it was there, pushing them back to the coast.

'Rückkehr zum Standort!'

Mission aborted, they sped to the safety of the North Sea.

At first no one at Mildenhall wanted to admit what they had seen. Bad enough that a witch was supposed to haunt Mum's

Wood – but this? A man who conjured a sandstorm from the still night air? Eventually the tale got out, and the people of Mildenhall told the airmen about the Guardian of the Brecks and how sometimes when a storm started up they had caught glimpses of him and his flute out of the corners of their eyes.

The airmen felt privileged to have seen so much more, and they took to calling him 'Old Roger', as if he was part of a crew.

As the war dragged on, it was easy to forget such things in the day-to-day mix of drudgery and danger. There were sandstorms aplenty, and men swore they'd glimpsed Old Roger.

Then the squadrons changed. 149 squadron was replaced by 75, a squadron of New Zealanders, and 115, from RAF Marham in Norfolk. 149 squadron told them about Old Roger, just in case.

By 1942 the coastal defences were so closely guarded that it was hard for enemy aircraft to penetrate inland. But one dark and cloudy night, a lone bomber slipped over the defences and chuntered away towards Mildenhall. No one noticed it go by. The low cloud muffled the Dornier's sound, and hid it from view. None of the airfields along the way, not Halesworth or Metfield, not Eye or Honington, noticed it was there.

Only when the threatening rumble of the Dornier sounded over the clearer skies of the Breckland was Mildenhall alerted. The men scrambled to see it off, but as they raced to their planes, someone shouted out, 'What's that?'

'A Dornier 217, you fool!' cried someone else through the mirk.

'No – listen!'

There, once more, was the sound of a low flute and then the whistle of the wind.

'It's Old Roger! Everyone – get inside, get inside!'

The barracks doors were closed just as the sandstorm hit. A sheet of sand slammed over the airfield and was on the lone bomber before its crew had time to register the threat. The plane turned and fled, but the sandstorm paced it, mile for mile, back past Shepherd's Grove, Mendlesham and Framlingham, until at last the storm caught it. The bomber plummeted from the sky and crashed into the claggy fields.

When the plane was found, the RAF investigators were surprised at what they saw. The Dornier's engines were filled with sand. These men, unfamiliar with the county's northern landscapes, were puzzled.

'No wonder it came down.' said one. 'You'd think it had been flying across the desert, not Suffolk. I've not seen anything like it since I was in Egypt in 1940. Sandstorms like this in Suffolk! Unheard of.'

But when the news came back to RAF Mildenhall, the crews knew exactly how the sand had got into the plane. That night in the mess, everyone raised a glass to Old Roger, the Guardian of the Breckland.

Suffolk had no less than thirty-two airfields during World War II, and there are many tales of strange happenings during the course of the war. Mildenhall was the most famous of the bases, and even featured in a film, Target for Tonight *(1941), in which the airfield was cunningly disguised as 'RAF Millerton'.*

FIFTEEN

THE SUFFOLK MIRACLE

John Haward was a rich farmer from Layham who had one child, Betty. The farmer loved his daughter and was determined that she would rise in the world. She was pretty, hard-working and good-natured, and he dreamed of her marrying someone far better than another farmer. In his mind's eye he saw her ensconced at the local manor, Moat Hall, and imagined himself dangling an aristocratic grandson on his knee.

Haward said nothing of his ambition to Betty. She divided her time between supervising the dairymaids, working in the still room and making fine embroidery like a real lady. But the highlight of her week was to go to market at Hadleigh with her parents. When she was a child she had loved the puppets and the storytelling and the chance of a new toy; but now she was older, and there were other things to amuse her.

All the young men in the area came to Hadleigh for market day, but there was only ever one man for Betty. As soon as she saw him with his thick golden hair, his broad shoulders and his smiling face, she knew that Joseph Henry was the man for her. As for Joseph, when he saw Betty with her long blond locks and her laughing blue eyes, he was just as smitten. There wasn't a market day when the two wouldn't find a little time to be together. Joseph made it clear to Betty that his intentions were honourable and that as soon as he could afford it they would marry.

Joseph knew that he wasn't the kind of man that Betty's father wanted: everyone save Betty knew that Farmer Haward had ideas above his station. But he talked to his father, and it was agreed that Joseph would go into partnership with him, and his father gave him the small sum of money he'd set aside long ago for his son's wedding day.

'People'll always want their horses shod and their tools mending,' said his father. 'Your bride'll never want for anything, no matter what that man says, so you hold your ground and hold your head high.'

Joseph went to Layham, and Farmer Haward's farm. The farmer was surprised to see the young blacksmith, but he received him in the parlour without a qualm. But when Joseph made his speech about how he loved Betty and she loved him Haward's fury grew and grew.

'How dare you come here and ask me this?' he cried. 'Are you such a fool that you can't see she's far too good for the likes of you? You can offer her nothing. Get out and never darken my doors again! I'd see her dead before she marries a blacksmith. You can be sure I'll never let you see her again.'

When Betty saw her lover arrive, she'd run to her mother and told her that soon she would be married. Betty's mother had known that her daughter held a candle to someone, but she knew her husband well and she shook her head.

'Joseph Henry is a fine young man, daughter, and some might say it was a fine match, but you may rest assured that you will never be his wife while your father lives.'

Betty wouldn't believe it, even when she saw Joseph walking away from the house with his head bowed.

Then her father was up the stairs and in her room and shouting, 'You little hussy! Carrying on with one such as him. I should take my belt to you!'

'Father, I love him! Don't you want me to be happy?'

'Happy tightening your belt and counting the pennies? No, my girl, you will put that good-for-nothing from your head and forget him. You'll not be seeing him again. Now, pack your bags!

I'm sending you to your uncle in Cambridge and you'll not come home until you've forgotten that blacksmith!'

Betty wept and begged and shouted and cajoled, but it was no good. Before the morning was out, she was sitting on her father's cart with her cases strapped to the back, being driven away from the farm towards Cambridge.

As she and her father's man drove through the lanes, she hardly noticed the tall oak and ash hedges heavy with elderflower, bramble and roses, the frothing cow parsley and buttons of tansy, gay on the banks. The fields were dancing with poppies and cornflowers, the drowsy curves of the cow pasture flattening out to a wide horizon of ripening corn as they went north, past Stowmarket, past Bury, and into the fenland with its swaying reeds as they neared Cambridge. Betty hardly saw the changes, and throughout the journey she never spoke a word.

She was left at her uncle's house with her cases and a letter from her father. Her uncle and her aunt were delighted to see her, but when her uncle read the letter his heart sank. His brother was a fool to expect that his daughter would marry so well, he thought, and he wished he dared send her straight back home to marry the worthy young blacksmith. But he was the younger brother, and he dared not.

Back in Hadleigh, Joseph cursed himself for being weak. The very next day, he went back to the farm to demand the girl he loved, and to spirit her away if he had to. But when he got there he found she was gone. Farmer Haward spun a tale of how glad she'd been to go and how she'd chattered of the fine young scholars she'd meet in Cambridge.

Joseph went home defeated again, but he waited to be proved wrong, waited for a letter or some word that his Betty truly loved him. But no word came. Joseph stopped working and took to his bed. He turned away food, he turned away drink, and soon he was truly ill. His parents sent for the doctor, but there was nothing anyone could do.

Within a month Joseph was dead.

When news came to Farmer Haward he was shocked, and he wondered if he had been wrong. Guilt propelled him to the funeral, but he didn't dare go in the church, and when the mourners came out they ignored him.

By the time he was home again he'd convinced himself that it was for the best. When his wife said that they should go and fetch their daughter, or at least write to tell her the bad news, he refused.

'Better if she stays a little longer and forgets him,' he said.

His wife was sure she would not forget, but she kept her peace.

In Cambridge, Betty's aunt and uncle were nothing but kind to her. They tried to entice her with parties and fine food, but she remained silent and grew thin and pale. Every day, when she should have been saying her prayers, she begged Joseph to come for her. A month passed, and another, with no word from him at all. But when that second month was nearly spent, the household was woken in the dead of night by a knocking at the door.

It was her uncle who answered. In the doorway stood a young man holding the reins of an exhausted, foaming horse. Even in the dim candlelight, the uncle could see how thin and pale this young man looked.

'I have come for Betty,' said the young man in a hollow voice. 'We'll not be parted again.'

There was a cry from upstairs and down flew Betty, her face alight with joy.

'Joseph, Joseph, you've come! My father has given consent!'

The young man stared at her, but he didn't smile.

'We must leave,' he said. 'We have a long journey home. I have your father's fastest horse and your mother's hood and safeguard to keep you warm.'

Her uncle was all for keeping him there the night, but the young man just stood and waited as Betty ran to dress. He could only watch as she put on the hood and wrapped the safeguard over her skirts.

Then she was up behind Joseph on the horse and away.

Cambridge was soon left behind; the horse flew over the ground so fast it took her breath away. Under the moon the cornfields seemed flat and dead. The earth was still and silent; not even an owl hooting and not a wisp of wind. Joseph was so silent, and when she wrapped her arms around his waist he was so cold, so cold, and she shivered as they rode.

At last they slowed, and Joseph turned to her.

'My head aches so.' His voice was so hollow. He seemed so far away and lost.

Betty tried to make light of her fear. 'And no wonder,' she said. 'All this riding in the cold night air!'

She took off the kerchief from her neck and tied it around his head. As she did her hand brushed his cheek – and she had to snatch it away. He was cold, so cold it burned. She looked at his still face and his solemn eyes and she hardly knew him. Fear rose in her. But she shook herself and said, 'We'll have you by the fire as soon as we are back in Layham.'

It took only two hours to cover the forty miles from Cambridge to Layham. When they arrived at her father's house in the grey light of dawn, Joseph helped her off the horse and then kissed her once. His lips were as cold as the clay, and the scent of the earth was on him.

The soft, chill touch tingled on her lips as she watched him lead the horse to the stable. Then she knocked on the door.

Her father answered – and stood stock still in shock to see his daughter there.

'How – what are you doing here?' he cried.

Betty looked up at him puzzlement.

'But, father, didn't you send for me yourself? You sent your fastest horse and my mother's hood and safeguard. You sent my Joseph to me and he came.'

Farmer Haward's hair stood on end. He led his daughter inside, sat her down in her bedchamber, and told her that they would all talk in the morning. He watched as she slumped on her bed, exhausted.

Then he raced out to the stable, but there was no sign of Joseph; just his fastest horse safe in his stall, but covered with lather as if he had been ridden all night. Haward saddled up his grey mare and rode to Hadleigh. He went straight to the house of the blacksmith, and begged him to come.

When Betty awoke, her father and Joseph's father were sitting at her bedside.

'Where is Joseph?' she cried – and she told her tale again. 'He only went to stable the horse, and he was cold, so cold, even though I had given him my kerchief.'

The two men said nothing. In grim silence, their differences forgotten in their horror, they rode back to Hadleigh and roused the churchwarden. The three of them went to the churchyard and dug open the grave. There in the grave lay Joseph, and he was as a corpse of one month should be – but around his head was a fresh linen kerchief with Betty's fine embroidery on it.

Farmer Haward went back to his daughter. By now she was frantic. He could hardly bear to tell her that her lover was a month dead. At first she would not believe it. She touched her lips, which still tingled with Joseph's clay-cold kiss. She did not weep; she lay down on her bed and turned her face to the wall.

Within the week she was dead.

They buried her in Hadleigh churchyard beside Joseph. Her father lived to a great age, and not a day passed that he didn't come to their grave to beg forgiveness that he had not allowed them their love.

'The Suffolk Miracle' is a well-known ballad featured in many collections. The version I have adapted is from The Suffolk Garland *of 1818. Broadsides of this song were published in the seventeenth century in Woodbridge. There are many beliefs surrounding the dead, and many practices were designed to ensure that the soul would go on and not linger among the living. It was thought that dwelling too much on the dead would cause them to return, and this invariably doomed the griever as well.*

SIXTEEN

THE ITALIAN

John Liffen was born and bred a Gritster. He was born on Anguish Street in the Beach Village in Lowestoft, the eldest child of eleven, most of them girls. He knew he'd work the yawls like his father one day, fishing down the East Anglian coast. For now, though, he was too young, not yet strong enough to work the boats. Even so, he had to work. His father drank his wages away, and with eleven children John's mother had little time for work.

He took any job he could get, but the gasworks gave him the most work. He sweated there every day to feed the fires to power the town. At the end of a long day there he'd take his wages straight home and put them in his mother's hand. Then he'd run down to Ness Point, strip off his clothes and plunge into the cold North Sea to wash away the grit and the grime and the long hours of toil. He'd swim straight out to sea, dreaming of the lands so close over the water at this, England's eastern-most point. Someday he'd get over there, he told himself. Someday.

His father was away for weeks at a time. One night John came in and there was his father, filling their one small downstairs room full of his evil pipe smoke. Last time he'd been back, Tom Liffen had spent most of his leave in the Waggon and Horses. As John stepped shyly into the room he thought his father looked surprised to see him.

'Is that you, John? You're nearly a man! You'll be joining me on the Daisy Sue before too long.'

John said nothing, but inside he was beaming.

His father strode across the room to clap John on the back.

'You're a man, right enough. And I think it best if you get a little initiating tonight! Mary, don't wait up for us. I'm taking the boy to the Waggon and Horses.'

John opened his mouth to protest, to say that he didn't want to catch the drinking habit, but his father had his hand firmly on his shoulder and was propelling him out of the door and down the street before he could speak. Never mind. His father had said he was a man, and so, for tonight at least, he'd be a drinking man.

His father ushered him into the pub, where the lad was greeted with jests and hair ruffling. A pint was drawn for him, and for a few glorious minutes he was the centre of his father's attention. The cool, bitter liquid slid easily down his throat and amidst the camaraderie of the fishermen he understood for a moment what drew his father here night after night.

It didn't last. Once Tom had a couple of pints in him, he seemed to forget that John was there. Quietly John withdrew to an empty table in the shadows by the window, sipped his drink, and wondered how long he would have to wait before he could slip away unnoticed.

'Scusi? This chair, it is taken?'

John looked up with a start. Standing over him was a man with a tanned face and oiled black curls. For a moment John looked into the man's eyes, and felt himself spiralling away. His father's neglect suddenly pressed hard on his soul, and anger burned in him. He tore his eyes away and took a large swig of his drink. And choked. The man laughed and slapped him on the back.

'First time?'

John nodded, then remembered his manners and gestured for the man to sit. The man sprawled in the seat, instantly at ease, and swirled the beer in his glass.

'I am Nicolò – I come in last week, on the Piccolo Diavolo. And you? Drinking alone, so young? You have troubles?'

John started to shake his head, but the man looked so sympathetic that everything tumbled out: his family's poverty, his father's drinking, his own stupid youth that stopped him from bringing in a good

wage; the itch to leave the Beach. The Italian nodded and made all the right noises until he was finished, then before John could be embarrassed the man fetched him another drink and smiled.

'When I was a boy, I too long to travel…'

For the rest of the evening John listened, spellbound, as the Italian regaled him with tales of his adventures. From that moment on, John and Nicolò were inseparable. Every night after work John would meet his friend and listen to his stories. They awakened in him such a hunger to leave that he could hardly bear it, but he handed his wages over to his mother and tried to carry on living as before.

One evening the Italian sat down beside him with a serious expression on his face.

'Giovanni, it is time. I leave tomorrow.'

John sagged in his seat, shocked.

'No, Giovanni, you do not understand. I have an offer. You will come with me and I will show you the world, as my apprentice. Those cities, those ports – we will go there, you and I.'

John couldn't believe his ears. He opened his mouth to accept the offer, but then his mother's tired face rose up in front of him. How could he leave her? If he left, that would be half their income gone, and his next brother was only eight years old.

'I can't,' he blurted. 'My mum, she needs me —'

He glanced up at Nicolò, and flinched from the fierce anger he saw in his eyes. But in a flash it was gone, and the Italian was smiling again.

'Va bene, then you will look after my dog while I am gone.'

John blinked. He hadn't known the Italian had a dog, but looking after it wouldn't be hard. He agreed. The Italian pressed a purse into his hand, then without a word, he got up and left.

John walked home in a daze. Without having even looked in the purse, he handed it to his mother. When she opened it she gasped.

'Where did you get this?'

John looked into the purse, then back at his mother in wonder.

'It was the Italian,' he said. 'He's leaving – he asked me to go with him, and – and I couldn't, not now. So he asked me to look after his dog.'

John's mother gave him a sad look as if she understood how hard it had been to say no.

'He's very generous,' she said.

Outside, there came a bark, and they both jumped. John went to the door, and there, sitting on the step and wagging his tail, was an enormous black dog.

'So it was true,' he said. 'He does have a dog.'

After that, it was the dog who was John's constant companion. He'd be waiting for John when he finished work, and he'd be there at the house in the morning when he set out. He was huge – came up to John's waist – but he was gentle with John, all lolling tongue and smiling eyes.

John welcomed the dog into his heart, yet he dwelt on the Italian's departure and his own lost dreams. One day, with the dog faithfully trotting alongside him, he was drawn to the beach at Ness Point. He stripped off, plunged into the cold water and swam out in the direction of the Continent. After swimming a distance, he stopped, began to tread water and then nearly sank under the waves when the black dog appeared from under the water.

'Hey boy!' he cried. 'You gave me a start! You didn't have to follow me.'

The dog just stared and, to John's astonishment, raised his hackles and began to growl.

'Easy now, boy. What's wrong?'

The dog kept growling.

'Time to go back, anyhow,' John muttered, and struck out towards the shore, hoping the stupid dog would follow.

Suddenly the dog was in front of him, blocking his way. John tried to push the dog away, but it wouldn't go. Then it snapped at him. John felt a chill that had nothing to do with the cold water. He wheeled in the water and tried to swim away, but again the dog was at him, growling and snapping.

Whichever way he turned, the dog was at him, and John realised that it was pushing him further and further out to sea. The look in its black eyes curdled a cold lump of fear in his belly. He had no choice but to keep swimming out to sea, and with every stroke the waves grew bigger. He was starting to tire. He had to get back!

Once more he tried to push back past the dog. He must have been getting very tired, because for a moment he saw not the dog but the Italian in front of him, with eyes like burning coals and a mocking smile. Then the dog was on him. There was blood in the water and a searing pain in his right shoulder. He watched in horror as the dog gulped down the gobbet of his flesh and came at him again. For a moment John trod water, unbelieving. Then, from God knows where, he summoned up energy and began to swim as fast as he could away from the dog, not caring in which direction he swam.

The yawl Dainty Maid was just preparing to come into Lowestoft, when one of the men spotted a waving arm, and cried out, 'Christ, there's a boy in the water!'

John was hauled up, shaking and bleeding, onto the deck. For a moment he lay there panting, but then, ignoring the shouts of the sailors, he dragged himself to the side. In the water he saw the black dog. Its eyes burned at him with hate, then it plunged down, like a porpoise, under the waves. John stared at the sea until someone gave a shout, and he turned and saw a black shape in the distance swimming off towards the Netherlands.

John was brought safely home. His wound healed. Soon after, his father came home and declared that John was old enough to start working the boats. For many long years, John was a fisherman. He accepted the work as his due, working hard and soberly, giving his wages first to his mother and then to his wife. But sometimes he would go to Ness Point and stare out to sea, and wonder.

He never mentioned the dog or the Italian again. But the story of the dog wouldn't go away. Men said it still haunted the streets, and John saw how they would look sideways at him when they spoke of it.

And sometimes, even after John died, a boy's body would be washed up on Ness Point. People would speak of inexperienced swimmers, but they couldn't explain the tooth marks on the bodies, as if a dog had savaged them, far out to sea.

The Beach Village or 'the Grit' in Lowestoft is all but gone now, its houses and streets transformed into factories and carpet showrooms. In its heyday more than 2,500 people lived there. Anguish Street started out as 'Anquish Street', named after the lord of the manor in the mid-nineteenth century, Revd George Anquish. The name was swiftly changed, reflecting the mordant humour of the Gritsters.

SEVENTEEN

THE
SILLY SAINTS

The first cathedral in East Anglia was at South Elmham. It is said that St Felix was impressed by the pure faith and simple lives of the folk who lived in the area. Felix was a man who understood the corruptions of power and commerce, and he longed to keep this one corner of his flock in a pure state. He told them that they should concentrate on praising God, that they should not build roads and should not mix with the heathen folk that still surrounded them in ungodly places like Halesworth and Bungay. The people took his injunctions to heart.

A group of villages grew up, in scattered Suffolk fashion, near the cathedral. There were once thirteen churches in the Elmhams and Ilketshalls, and so the area became known as 'the Saints'. The godliness might have faded, but they kept themselves to themselves as commanded. From rumours of treacle mines at nearby Wissett to the howling demon under Homersfield bridge, a reputation for strangeness grew up in the area.

One night, a labourer was walking home from St James to St Michael under the light of a fat full moon. On his way, he had to cross the damp green at All Saints, and he skirted close to the pond by the road. Through the willows, he caught a glimpse of something pale in the water, and went to investigate.

A white and perfectly round cheese floated there. Suffolk cheese was nothing to write home about, but this cheese looked to be foreign, and he could almost taste its salty, tangy yumminess. It was floating right in the centre of the pond, but he didn't have anything with which to reach it.

There was a thatched cottage immediately opposite, so off he ran and banged on the door.

'There's a cheese in your pond! Help me get it out and we'll have ourselves a feast!'

The sleepy farmer grabbed a hoe and went and knocked on all the doors of All Saints. Soon there was a whole posse heading to the pond. There the cheese still floated, just at the surface. But it was strange; no sooner did someone touch with it their hoe or rake than it would disappear under the water. As soon as the tool was withdrawn, up the cheese would bob. One chap even waded in, but as soon as he got close enough to touch it, down it went. For all his searching, it wouldn't come up until he was gone.

All night they tried to raise it, getting wetter and wetter, and all night the cheese eluded them. At last, near dawn, a great cloud covered the sky, and it was too dark to see. The villagers and our labourer all shook their heads and headed for home.

'That's a rum'un alright. That'll spoil now,' they said. 'That's wholly been in the water too long.'

Sure enough, in the morning the cheese was gone.

The people of St James, when they heard the story, how they laughed. They declared that they'd never be duzzy old fools like those folk from All Saints, and think the moon a cheese! But, in truth, a cheese would have been a fine thing that year, as the harvest had been poor and there was a fair bit of belt-tightening come spring.

A group of farmers were sitting under a tree bemoaning the situation when they heard the first cuckoo of summer.

'That's right!' cried one. 'If we keep the cuckoo all year round we'd have summer all year long. It do stand to reason. Cuckoo brings the summer, so if we keep the cuckoo, we'll have summer all year long, and then we'll have two, three, maybe four harvests a year!'

The villagers all agreed that this was a very sensible notion, and they scoured the bushes and the hedges in search of a young cuckoo, reckoning that catching a baby would be easier. They found the ideal candidate in a weary dunnock's nest in a hedge by a farm, close up by the church. That dunnock worked hard for her interloper chick, but the villagers helped, and soon the cuckoo chick grew fat on the titbits the villagers brought.

Soon it was clear the bird was getting ready to fly, and the villagers began to get worried. So they built up the hedge all around with hurdles until it stood far taller than the nest. They watched and waited, and sure enough, the cuckoo lifted its wings and flew – straight up and out of the hedge. The villagers of St James watched it fly up into the sky.

'That's wholly gone!' they cried. 'We didn't build our hedge high enough.'

And the winter came that year as winters always do.

Sometimes the only solace a Saints man could find was in the drink. And the best place for that was the Buck at Rumburgh. One night, it drew a bunch from St Michael, and they found their steps weaving a bit on their way home. One lad was so far gone that he wandered ahead of his friends, sipping from his little hipflask. His friends watched him go, and started to whisper to each other how they might trick him before he got safe home.

When our man got to St Michael's church, he stopped dead. That hadn't been like that when he left, he was sure.

Pointing at the tower, he cried, 'that's on the huh!'

St Michael's tower wasn't tall, but somehow, between him going to the pub and coming back, it had got out of kilter.

'That'll never do. I'll put that right!'

He took off his coat and set it down against the tower wall. Then he rolled up his sleeves, set his shoulder to the tower and heaved. And heaved.

His friends had heard the whole thing. They weren't going to look a gift horse in the mouth, and an idea for a trick quickly formed. One of their number ran into the churchyard on tippy-toes and snatched their chum's coat. Then off they ran, almost bursting with laughter.

The man was too intent to notice. Each heave took the wind out of him, and he had to pause and reset his feet for each great effort. Slowly, he worked his way around the tower, and when he'd reached the other side, he looked up in satisfaction. The tower was as straight as it always had been.

So, smiling in the aftermath of a job well done, he reached down for his coat. But it wasn't there. He searched all around the wall, but there was no sign. He distinctly remembered setting it against the tower. Then it dawned on him. While he was putting the tower straight, he'd managed to set it down on his coat. That was how he'd got it straight – the coat was holding it up! He shivered, then shrugged. If that was what it took to make the church right, then it was a fair sacrifice to make. So headed home and the next day bragged to his friends and all the other villagers about how he'd fixed the church.

Most people were impressed, but his friends smiled to themselves and never revealed to him how they'd stolen his coat. The man lived to his dying day believing that the tower was held up by his coat.

These stories – moonraking, hedging the cuckoo, straightening or growing the church – are well known throughout the country. Most counties have a place where the 'sillies' live, and the same stories appear across the country. Suffolk has two such places: the Saints and Hadleigh – where I went to school! In fact, the whole of Suffolk is 'silly'. In this case 'silly' really means 'sele', an Anglo-Saxon word for 'holy', just as St Felix intended. And St Felix and the Saints have the last laugh: even in this age of sat-navs, it's still easy to get lost in the Saints.

EIGHTEEN

KING EDMUND

Old King Athelweard died in 854 with no heir. A young boy of the Wuffing line was chosen as new king. His name was Edmund, and he was only fourteen years old. Even as a youth, he impressed the thanes with his easy friendliness and natural diplomacy. The boy was whisked south to the royal capital at Bures St Mary by the Stour, and Bishop Hunberht of Elmham crowned him on Christmas Day in the chapel on the hill. It was a new beginning, folk said, for the coming of the new year.

Edmund was determined to be a good king. He studied state-craft and warcraft, met his thanes, travelled his kingdom. It was a heavy task for a young boy. His greatest friend was a young man of his own age, his Danish huntsman Bern. The two were insepa-rable and would go out into the reed-beds near the royal villa at Reedham to hunt wildfowl. These short escapes from his kingship with his devoted friend gave Edmund great pleasure. He found another friend in Bishop Hunberht, who encouraged his religious studies. For a year, at the monastery at Iken, Edmund translated the psalter into his own tongue, so he might praise the Lord better.

He grew to be a careful, thoughtful young man. His people came to love him for his fair and just rule. But it was not an easy time to be King. For years the Northmen had come a-viking, raiding British shores, but now there was talk of conquest and bloodshed across the water in France. All England waited in fear, and in 865 the Great Heathen Army struck. First, a lightning attack in Kent, which brought the Kentish King to his knees, and then up the coast and into East Anglia. Edmund knew that this was no raiding party. He sent men to test the Danes' mettle. None of those men returned. Edmund knew what he had to do. A gift of the kingdom's finest horses was proffered, and Ivar the Boneless and his men departed northwards to claim the great prize of Northumbria.

That was not the last of the Danes that East Anglia saw that year. In the winter, another boat came across the sea. A small boat, with one occupant. Edmund and Bern were out hunting in the reed-beds near the Waveney at Oulton Broad, and they heard a voice calling, 'Help, help, help!' They soon found the man – thin, grey-bearded, hollow-eyed and encrusted with salt. But at his shoulders were gold cloak clasps. Pauper or king, Edmund didn't care. He invited the man to feast at his hall at Reedham.

At the end of the meal, Edmund asked his guest who he was.

The old man fixed Edmund with his gaze, and said, 'I was hunting alone in my reed-beds across the sea. I drew too close to the sea; the current caught me and washed me away. Even my oars were snatched by the sea. At last I arrived on your shore, and received your hospitality. I am Ragnar Lothbrok. Perhaps you have heard of me?'

Indeed Edmund had. Ragnar was the greatest of the Danish pirates. Not only that; he was the father of Ivar the Boneless. A whole range of possibilities rose in Edmund's mind. But those thoughts were not Christian: he had given guest-rights to Ragnar.

'Be welcome, Ragnar,' he said. 'The sea-roads are not safe, so stay with us this winter. In the spring my trading ships will return to Denmark, and they will carry you home.'

Ragnar stayed, and he and the King became fast friends. Ragnar was a fine hunter, and the two would go into the reed-beds hunting wildfowl. Edmund's huntsman Bern watched the two men ride out each day, and burned with anger that he was left behind, he who was the King's dearest friend.

Late in the winter, Bern invited Ragnar to hunt with him. The two set off with only Ragnar's dog for company. Deep into the marshes they went, down by the River Waveney where only the widgeon and teal could hear them. Bern chased off Ragnar's dog. Then he drew his dagger and struck. Ragnar sank into the water. Bern held him under until he was sure the Dane was dead, then wedged the body in the reeds.

When Bern got home, Edmund asked after Ragnar.

Bern shrugged. 'He went his own way early on. I am not his minder, so I came home.'

At supper, Ragnar's dog limped home. Everyone said Ragnar would soon follow. But he did not. All night his dog kept vigil by the door, only to shoot off at first light. Edmund knew there was something wrong. He declared he would lead the search himself.

When Bern heard this he was filled with fear that his deed would be discovered. He insisted that he should lead. 'After all, was I not the last to see him?'

He took them far in the wrong direction. But Edmund heard the howling of a dog far off towards the river, and he set off alone, following the dog's howls. Soon enough he found him, and the body lodged in the reeds. He found the bloody wound and he guessed what had happened. He called out to his men, and when they caught up, Bern was with them and he saw that Edmund knew. He fell to his knees in the water and confessed.

Edmund knew that his men would expect Bern's death. But Bern was his dearest friend. He felt a stab of guilt that he had ignored Bern in favour of his new friend.

'God's will brought Ragnar among us, and so I give you to God to do with as he wishes.'

They brought Ragnar's small boat from its mooring and placed Bern in it. As Ragnar had had nothing, not even oars, so Bern was given no supplies. Then they took him to the mouth of Waveney and cast him out to sea.

'Think on what you have done, and pray for mercy. You are at God's mercy now. Go with him.'

For days Bern drifted, the roar of the sea constant in his ears, drear nothingness on all sides. Soon he was mad with it. He became filled with hate for Edmund. Better that he should have died than endure this! But at last he spotted land, and his little boat carried him into some reeds.

He walked until he came to a settlement and then asked whose land this was.

'This is Ragnar Lothbrok's land.'

Bern could not believe his ears, and a plan formed in his mind. He demanded to be taken to the hall of Ivar the Boneless, Ragnar's son.

'Your father has been slain,' he told Ivar. 'King Edmund took him in, granted him the gift of hospitality, but just as the seaways were opening, he killed your father. I, who spoke against it, was cast adrift on the sea.'

The three sons of Ragnar – Ivar, Halfdan and Hubba – swore vengeance. Halfdan and Hubba were for going to East Anglia straight away, ravaging the land, killing the King; but Ivar held up his hand.

'We have unfinished business in York. We will first take Northumbria and then kill this murderer. Revenge is a dish best eaten cold.'

The Great Heathen Army, with Ivar at its head, crossed the sea once more. They took the city of York, killed the Northumbrian King Aelle, subjugated Mercia and only then turned back to East Anglia. Word had come of Bern's deceit, and Edmund knew the Danes fought for vengeance. He prayed to God for guidance, but also amassed a huge army, and waited. Soon enough, Danes were spotted sailing down the coast, and Edmund's men raced to meet them when they landed.

Too late. The fleet came in at Orford, torched the houses, then sailed up the Butley river. Edmund saw the ships approaching and ordered his men to hide in the forest at Staverton. They watched the Danish army pour from the boats: a never-ending stream of warriors. The East Anglians were seen, and the Danes plunged into the forest after them.

The shouts of men echoed from tree to tree, calling to Odin, calling to God, the summer leaf cover so heavy that it was hard to see who was Angle or Dane. Under the shadow of the ancient, twisted oaks they fought, and with every clash the East Anglians were pushed back.

'Retreat,' cried Edmund.

The East Anglians hightailed towards High Suffolk and the great fortress at Framlingham. They barricaded themselves in and waited for the Danes to arrive.

Ivar was not interested in a lengthy siege. He went into the village and questioned the terrified villagers. He soon found what he wanted, an old mason who had worked on the fortress. The man was old and blind.

Ivar pretended to be one of Edmund's own retainers. 'I am so worried that the Danes will find a flaw, a way in to the hall,' he whispered in the old mason's ear.

The man told him where there was a weakness in the walls.

Before Edmund knew it, the Danes were pouring into the fortress. For an instant he saw Ivar, and their gazes locked. Ivar's eyes were filled with fury. There would be no mercy there. Edmund knew he had to escape.

He fled, scrambling alone through the very hole that Ivar's men had made. He leapt onto the first horse he could find, and was away, racing across his kingdom, fleeing north until he came to the ford over the Waveney at Syleham, and then he was over the river and on to his hall at Thetford.

There he regrouped his men, but word came that the Danish ships were in pursuit up the coast, torching the villages as they went – even the monastery at Iken where Edmund had translated the psalter. Edmund's army marched out once more, following the Waveney. Just past Beccles they met the Danes again. There were so many of them, but the East Anglians knew the land; Edmund better than any, thanks to his youthful hunting trips with Bern.

Just as the Anglian victory shout went up, Edmund found himself alone by the river and surrounded by the Danes. Without thinking, he flung himself into the water and swam until he was hidden by the reeds, then he swam and ran until he came to a ford that he and Bern had found once as youths, and plunged across the river to safety.

It was a victory, but at such a cost. Most of Edmund's men were dead, and he knew he could not win the war. As if to prove him right, a message arrived from Ivar, one the Dane knew that Edmund couldn't accept.

'Submit to me, become my vassal king, and I will spare you and your land. Swear that you will honour me above all others, including your god.'

Even old Bishop Hunberht urged him to give in. 'Better a live vassal king who cares, my liege, than one of them ruling good Anglian souls.'

But Edmund would not put his immortal soul in such danger. And he knew in his heart that Ivar would not be content with such a small vengeance. Ivar would have him killed. It was just a question of when. So Edmund sent back a message saying, 'I will become your vassal when you become a Christian.'

The next they heard was that Ivar's army was marching towards Edmund at Thetford. Edmund mustered what few men he had and marched back across the Waveney to meet him. Their forces met near the village of Hoxne. It was a rout. Edmund fled into the village with a handful of survivors. Ivar and his men burnt the village as they searched for him.

The villagers fled. Farmers, women, children. Even a bride and groom fled from the burning church, away towards the groom's farm on the outskirts of the village. As they raced over the bridge over the Goldbrook, the sun came out, and they glimpsed something under the bridge. They looked down, and looking back up at them was a cluster of warriors. Thinking them more Danes, the woman screamed.

But they were not Danes. They were Edmund and his guard. At the woman's cry, Ivar's men came running. The King and his men were hauled out of their hiding place. The guard struggled to protect Edmund. The Danes fell on them, and soon cut them down.

Edmund stood alone, with only his young armour-bearer beside him.

He knew this was the end. He turned to the boy and hissed, 'Run! Hide! Someone must witness this. Someone must live to tell this story. Go!'

And with that, he turned towards Ragnar's sons and let his sword fall from his hand.

Hubba and Halfdan leapt forward with whoops of glee and grabbed the King. In the confusion the boy threw himself into the bushes by the stream and watched, trembling and sick with dread, as the Danes dragged the King away towards the wood on the edge of the village. He followed quietly behind and watched as they tied Edmund to a lone young oak tree in a field next to the wood.

At first they just flicked the King with their horsewhips. Edmund closed his eyes and began to recite the Lord's Prayer. Ivar hissed at him to stop, but Edmund just spoke louder. Ivar raised his spear and cast it at the King. Hubba and Halfdan followed suit, and soon Edmund was bristling with spears, like a hedgehog. He cast his eyes to the heavens and cried out, 'O Lord Jesus, have mercy on me! Give me the strength you had on the cross.'

Then Ivar slashed his bonds, and they dragged him, still stuck with spears, to the wood. There Ivar raised his sword and with one blow cut off Edmund's head. Hubba leapt forward and brandished the head.

'Odin!' cried Ivar. 'My father is avenged this day!'

Hubba raced deeper into the wood, and with a whoop threw the head deep into the brambles. Then they left, leaving the body where it lay.

The armour-bearer waited long till he dared go into the wood. When he came to Edmund's headless body, he wept. As gently as he could, he pulled out the spears that pierced it. Then he went and gathered the villagers, determined to find the King's head. But the head could not be found. The villagers said they should just bury the body – or else the blood would bring wolves.

The armour-bearer shook his head. All he could think of was his King's devotion to God, his courage in death, and how if his head were not reunited with his body, then at the day of resurrection he would not be able to rise with the righteous dead to take his place in the kingdom of God. So they searched the woods until nightfall. But the head was not to be found. All the next day they searched, and the next, and by the end of that third day the villagers would search no more.

Then, a voice from the wood cried, 'Here, here, here.'

The armour-bearer went white. 'That is the voice of my king.'

They followed the voice still calling 'Here, here, here,' until they came to a clearing.

The villagers stepped back in fear, because in front of them was an enormous grey wolf. Cradled between her paws was the King's head. She snarled at the villagers, but when the armour-bearer dared to step forward, she whined. When he reached her she stepped back, and he took Edmund's head and wrapped it carefully in a cloak.

The wolf followed ten paces behind them, all the way to the edge of the wood. There she sat down and lifted her muzzle to the air and howled. Her voice was soon joined by another and another until the twilight air echoed with the wolves' grief. In the gloom, the armour-bearer and the villagers buried Edmund under the tree where he had been martyred. They placed his head as best they could atop his body.

That was not quite the end. The fighting raged on, but soon enough East Anglia was defeated. The churches and monasteries were destroyed and Bishop Hunberht was slain. But the people's faith was strong. When the dust had settled, and the Danes' atten-

tion turned to Wessex, the faithful returned to Hoxne to build a shrine to the King. But when they dug up the body, it was as fresh as the day he died – and there was a miracle, for his head was once more attached to his shoulders; only a thin red line round his neck to mark the cut.

God had made his wishes known. King Edmund was a saint.

St Edmund was England's patron saint until 1348, when Edward III replaced him with St George. In 905 Edmund's body was translated from Hoxne to Bury St Edmunds. The saint became vengeful in death and protected his shrine with sometimes fatal results. The most famous instance was in 1014, when Sweyn Forkbeard was struck down by the saint for attacking the town. Even today people invoke his spirit for vengeance. The Knights of St Edmund formed in 2005 in protest against a new shopping centre in Bury and evoked St Edmund's curse. The failure of several businesses has been blamed on the curse. The Knights say they will not take back the curse until the shopping centre is pulled down. But Edmund may be slightly appeased – in 2006 he was made patron saint of Suffolk.

NINETEEN

THE WIZARD
OF IPSWICH

In 1744 the old Cunning Man of Ipswich died. His apprentice, a young lad by the name of Winter, took up the reins. This young man was Ipswich born and bred, and he lived in a tumbledown cottage on Foundation Street, opposite the Tooley Almhouses. Foundation Street was an up-and-coming place. Bold new façades with huge windows were popping up beside the crumbling plaster of timber-framed hovels, with a grammar school and workhouse nestling close by each other in the remains of the old Blackfriars. It was a street of contradictions: an ideal place for a new Cunning Man.

Winter was delighted with his new role, and not afraid to brag about it. He was a lad who made friends easily. But his first real test came soon after his master died. Garnham, a farmer who brought his sheep to market in Ipswich, sought Winter out and told him that he feared sorcery.

'It's that Mrs Pett of Angel Lane. Last market day I saw her looking funny-like at the sheep, and they've not bin right since.'

Winter said he would come and take a look. When he got to the farm it was plain what was wrong. The old Cunning Man had told him that it was the farmers on the edge of town who would give him the best business.

'Superstitious old boys, they are.'

He'd dragged Winter around the farms one year. Winter knew a good farm, and he knew a bad.

He was still young in his trade, and Garnham was burly and angry. Winter reckoned that to tell him that he was negligent would likely end in a beating. Instead, he checked the sheep thoroughly and then gave the farmer a long list of instructions.

'What about the magic?' cried Garnham.

Another lesson: remember to be impressive. Winter said some words over the sheep and drew some symbols on the floor.

'The sheep'll be right enough,' he said, 'if you follow the instructions.'

But the next week Garnham was back complaining about Mrs Pett. Winter went back and checked the sheep, laid down the same instructions and waited. But Garnham was persistent. On 8 April he came to where Winter was drinking with his friends and asked what Winter was going to do about the witch, as a sheep had died that day. Winter refused to curse Mrs Pett, but Garnham sat him down and plied him with drink until Winter caved in.

'She's no witch,' he slurred. 'Just a harmless fisherman's wife who likes a wee drink, and don't we all? But if you were to take a sheep and give it her name and burn it, then that would do the trick.'

Winter awoke the next morning in a cold sweat, knowing he'd done wrong. He hurried to Angel Lane where he saw Mrs Pett out with her two daughters, laughing away. He allowed himself to relax.

The following morning he was awakened by people hammering on his door. Mrs Pett's neighbours, begging him to come. When he arrived at her house in Angel Lane, a horrifying sight met him. All that remained of Mrs Pett was her two feet, still encased in their boots. But nothing else in the room was burnt, not even her own chair. There was no hint that a coal had leapt from the fire, and a candle stood pinched out on a shelf.

Her daughter was hysterical, saying that when she'd gone upstairs, her mother had been quietly smoking her pipe by the fire. The pipe was nowhere to be seen. When questioned, the daughter allowed that her mother liked a little drink before bed when her husband was out to sea.

Winter listened to everyone agree that it was a terrible accident, and then he slipped away, straight to Garnham's farm. The look on the farmer's face when he arrived told him all he needed to know – that and the dreadful smell of burning from the barn.

Winter threatened Garnham with a curse, and Garnham meekly took him to the barn. There in the middle of the floor was a sheep carcass. Or rather, the burnt remains of a sheep's feet.

Garnham looked at the floor. 'It was the wife. She got it into her head that the Pett woman was to blame, and she went and did it, just like you said. I'm sorry the old woman's dead. We just wanted to teach her a lesson.'

Winter went home and said no more about it, but someone on the farm must have told. The rumour grew that he'd been involved. He fully expected to be hauled up before the magistrate as a witch himself. But something unexpected happened. The incident made his reputation. People flocked to him, sure that his magic would work. Soon, he was the best-known Cunning Man in the whole of Suffolk. In his heart, though, he took an oath that he would never cause harm again. Instead he would right wrongs.

He got a name as a thief-taker. It all began when he was walking home up Fore Street late one night. He saw someone digging in one of the little gardens there. Winter knew whose plot it was. An old man and his wife grew a few vegetables there. They had no kin, but the figure in the garden seemed a vigorous young man. It was hard to tell in the darkness. So Winter waved his hand, and the man was frozen to the spot, his foot on his spade.

The next morning, Winter was up with the dawn. He quickly made his way back to Fore Street. A crowd had gathered and, sure enough, the young man was still there, wild-eyed and covered in dew with a pile of freshly dug vegetables as evidence beside him. Winter gave another wave of his hand and the young man was released, only to be taken briskly away by the authorities.

Winter's fame grew and grew. By the time he was in his fifties he was called out all over the county.

Once, a farmer near Stowmarket contacted him about some missing blocks of wood. After a fine meal from the farmer's wife,

Winter suggested after that he and the farmer should set themselves up by the window that overlooked the wood yard.

'Shouldn't we be out there, trying to catch the thief?' asked the farmer.

'He'll be caught, right enough,' said Winter. 'Why should we old folks have to exert ourselves for him? Now, you're not to speak a word until I give the word, no matter what you see.'

He settled back in his chair to wait.

About midnight, they were rewarded for their long vigil by the sight of a man walking into the moonlit yard. The farmer sat up and was about to speak, but Winter held up his hand and the farmer fell silent. The man was clearly a farm labourer – and from the farmer's black look, one he knew well. They watched as the man walked over to the wood pile and hefted a block of wood onto his shoulder.

As they watched him cross from the yard into the meadow behind, Winter was aware that beside him the farmer was nearly having an apoplexy. He held up his hand once more. This time he waved it in a certain way. The labourer, who had been marching purposely across the meadow, abruptly stopped and turned about as if he didn't know where he was.

The labourer began to pace the field, walking around and around, but seeming not to know where the way in or the way out was. Round and round he went, and it was clear to the two watchers that the wooden block was getting heavier and heavier as the man got slower and slower. Now the farmer was rocking back and forth in silent laughter.

Winter had seen enough. He gave the farmer a nod and they crept out into the yard. Through the gate into the meadow they went, until they were right next to the man. Even then he didn't seem to see them.

Winter waved his hand again.

The man clocked them, dropped the block and fell to his knees. They marched him to his house and found a whole stack of blocks in the labourer's own yard. Winter went home the next day with a sense of a job well done, and also a young apprentice to train up – the labourer's eldest son.

The years went by, and after he'd trained an apprentice or two, Winter started to think about retirement. Ipswich was changing. By the time he was in his eighties Winter found the hustle and bustle a bit much. He handed on the Ipswich trade to an apprentice, left Foundation Street and moved to Aldeburgh.

As old as he was, he couldn't quite bear to give up his life's work. He made himself useful to the Aldeburgh farmers by showing them how to keep the ferishers from riding the cattle, and by drawing symbols at the doors to keep out bad witches. A ploughman he discovered stealing cattle was turned upside-down and sent out to plough standing on his head. Thanks to this, the farmer was able to identify the culprit.

By then Winter knew exactly how to milk the mystery of his profession. The farmer and his young son came to pay their respects to the old man after Winter had caught the ploughman. The boy peeped round the door of the wizard's house before he and his dad were announced. He froze at what he saw. Old Winter was dozing in his chair, but there, on the table, danced half a dozen tiny black imps! To the boy they seemed half rat and half bat. He whimpered and tried to pull away from the door.

The old wizard seemed to start at that, and the boy heard him whisper, 'Get along with you now.'

The devils jumped off the table and glided down to the floor, chittering and giggling all the way, and then vanished into it.

Winter smiled and called in the boy's father. The farmer pulled his boy in, and the lad stood quivering by the table. Winter said a few polite words to the farmer and accepted the pie, cheeses and butter that had been brought in thanks for the dealing with the ploughman. Then he caught the boy's eye and gave him an unmistakable wink.

> *Old Winter is the most famous of Suffolk's cunning men and women. The stories relate his power and the respect people had for him; but most witch and wizard stories are more negative, like Garnham's attitude towards poor Mrs Pett. The belief in witches in Suffolk has been tenacious: the last ducking of a witch in Suffolk happened in 1825, and many people still today hang up hagstones – perhaps still to keep the witches out.*

TWENTY

BODIES ON THE BEACH

Late August 1940; the sea was alive with fire, and plumes of black smoke billowed up beyond the long shingle beach. The line of cottages on the shore looked on blankly, their residents evacuated weeks before. Urgent messages from the Bawdsey RADAR base alerted the soldiers based at Shingle Street that Operation Sea Lion was underway. The soldiers knew what to do. Oil was sent rushing down the pipelines out to sea, then ignited in a mass of flame. The fire roared loud over the sea, but not so loud that it drowned the sound of the screaming.

Those who were there would never forget those flames or those screams. And how could you forget the stench of burning bodies or the reek of boiling oil? Standing there and watching the sea burn, none of them felt heroic, even though they knew this was what they had to do. Their dreams would be haunted for the rest of their days. It was a secret that each man knew he had to take to his grave. No one must know, they were told, that Britain might have fallen to a German invasion that night.

In Aldeburgh, off-duty servicemen were enjoying a Saturday night dance in the Jubilee Hall, laughing with the young women and forgetting the war for an hour or two. It was a quiet night – not a single aircraft had been heard. But before the dance could really get going, the music was turned off and a Lieutenant stepped up on the stage.

'All of you off-duty, your leave is cancelled. Hope you enjoyed the dance, lads. You're back on duty again! Get yourselves ready – cars have been requisitioned to transport you.'

No one said where they were being taken, but Crabbe Street was only a couple of streets from the beach, and as they spilled from the hall they saw that the sky was alight with a red glow, as if the end of the world was coming.

'Best keep quiet about that,' said the Lieutenant. 'Remember, there's a war on.'

After an hour of hanging around and watching the fire, smoke and explosions in the sky, the order came that the men were to be stood down again.

'You lucky lads!' cried the Lieutenant. 'Your mates out there have got it all in hand, just so you can get dancing again!'

Everyone piled back inside, and the music started again. Anything to get away from that flaming sky.

At Bawdsey, just a mile or so south of Shingle Street, it was harder to escape the flames. Most people were asleep behind their blackouts, but Bob Dunn was up late having his tea. His house was on the cliff by the sea. As he did every night, he went outside to have a quiet smoke. But no sooner had he stepped outside than the cigarette slipped from his fingers as he stared at the burning sea, up the coast towards Shingle Street. Transfixed, he stayed and watched as the fire burned and smoke plumed black into the sky. Here and there, caught up among the flames, he was sure he could see ships.

When at last he went to bed, the flames danced behind his eyes. At first light, still awake, he got up and made his way down the road to the beach. A lorry was parked right down by the beach, covered in khaki tarp. The back end of tarp was rolled up, and there were soldiers busy hefting something into the back of the lorry.

They didn't notice him, so he kept walking until he could see the beach. Once more, he stopped in his tracks. On the beach lay many, many bodies, all blackened and burnt. As he watched, the soldiers gathered up some of them and slung them in the back of the lorry. He must have made a noise, for a sergeant looked up and then came racing up the track towards him.

'Oi! What are you doing here?'

'I live here.' Dunn gestured back up the cliff.

The sergeant glared up at the houses there and pursed his lips, as if living there was a crime.

'Well, remember this. You've seen nothing here. We weren't here, and neither were you. Now get out – and remember there's a war on!'

Down in Felixstowe, soldiers stationed at Landguard Fort were roused and told to get down to the beach. When they got there, they found it littered with bodies. Bodies that were blackened and burnt, but still clearly wearing Wehrmacht uniforms.

'Get these out of here,' called their sergeant. 'Then forget about it! Never mention this to anyone – or there'll be a court martial for you!'

The men muttered among themselves as they loaded the grizzly remains into lorries.

'Not just a raiding party, eh?'

'Hardly – look at 'em all. This was an *invasion*.'

The war moved on. But at the Co-op Funeral Service, even in 1941 and 1942, there would be the occasional call-out to remove *something* from the beaches along the Suffolk coast. But nobody said a word about it. After all, there was a war on.

After the war, when the residents of Shingle Street were allowed back home, they looked at their looted homes, the cracked concrete roads, the forlorn beach, and they shook their heads. Then Bill Friend discovered a MoD bunker in his garden.

'Leave it be, Bill,' said his wife. 'Heaven only knows what's in there.'

'Come on, now,' said Bill. 'Surely I've a right to know what's on my own land!'

When he broke in he didn't find much, just some boxes. But when he prised them open, the musty scent of burning filled the air. From the boxes he pulled burnt German uniforms. He alerted the authorities, and soldiers came and took the boxes away, then sealed up the bunker.

'You keep out of there, and forget about it,' they said.

But no one quite forgot – and no one told, either. Rumour and hearsay kept the story going. Even today at Shingle Street and Bawdsey, when the tide and the weather are right, a layer of blackened beach is revealed, and bits of molten metal can be found lurking under the pebbles.

Is this a folktale? For more than seventy years the rumour has stayed strong that the Germans tried to invade the relatively poorly protected East Anglian coast in 1940. Everyone involved was sworn to secrecy, but since the 1990s accounts have been trickling out. The files for Shingle Street were opened in 1992, but didn't mention the fires or bodies, only mustard gas experiments in the village. However, boats for Operation Sea Lion did start massing on the other side of the Channel, and there were certainly experiments with oil pipelines in Kent. But were there really bodies on the beach at Shingle Street?

TWENTY-ONE

THE FOOLISH SACRISTAN

Brother Hugh of Bury was delighted when he learnt who had been chosen as the new prior of his house of Austin Friars at Clare. Prior Wilfred's rule would be very different from pious Prior John's. Wilfred was an ambitious man, but he certainly wasn't pious. His great passion was hunting, not praying. It was common knowledge that his family had bought him the position, and everyone knew that Wilfred wouldn't rest until his priory was the foremost in the diocese. Hugh didn't care about that. Like Wilfred, he'd never wanted to be a friar, but with an elder brother inheriting his father's estates there was no other choice for him. Now he believed he would have the chance to indulge himself as he had always wanted.

Hugh was the Sacristan. He was in charge of the fine vessels, reliquaries and vestments belonging to the priory. Only Hugh had the key to the huge carved vestment chest and the great iron chest in which the church plate was kept. It became all too easy for Hugh to slip out a silver cup or a gold plate and pawn it in Clare for ready cash. He had lacked money all his life – until now. He spent more and more time in the town, eating succulent meals at the Moon Inn and sometimes sampling the upstairs fare offered at other, less illustrious, brewhouses.

But once he had begun, it was hard to stop. There was no other money coming in. To get one piece back, he had to pawn another, and as he always spent more than he had, it always had to be a finer piece than before. By now the other friars were starting to make comments about Hugh's frequent absences. Hugh was careful never to mention his misdemeanours even in confession. Instead he confessed to very minor sins like sleeping late or a small overindulgence at the dinner table. But all the time he – and God – knew there were gaping holes in the sacristy.

While Hugh frittered away the priory's treasures, Prior Wilfred was busy amassing more. His most recent piece was a finely embroidered cope from Edmund Mortimer, the priory's main benefactor. This was handed over to Hugh, who placed it lovingly in the vestment chest and eyed its fine workmanship with a greedy eye. Before the week was out, the cope was pawned and Hugh was enjoying his finest feasts yet.

Wilfred had bigger fish to fry than mere riches, however. The news around the county was that a papal ambassador was coming to the abbey at Bury. Wilfred had every intention of making sure the ambassador came to Clare, with all its royal connections and then – well, the clerical world would be Wilfred's oyster. No more rustication in rural Suffolk for him, and riches for Clare! One night he stood up at dinner and announced that he was going to Bury to invite the papal ambassador to the priory, and that when the ambassador came he would be given the new embroidered cope. Hugh nearly fainted on the spot.

The next day Prior Wilfred rode away to Bury.

Hugh panicked. He had to get the cope back. But there was nothing else so valuable in the sacristy. If he pawned lots of things someone would be bound to notice. He didn't know what to do, and so did nothing. The longer Prior Wilfred's stay in Bury went on, the more miserable Hugh became. He lost his appetite, and even took to prayer. The other brothers teased him about his new piety. Hugh was desperate, and when news came that Prior Wilfred would be back by the end of the week, and the papal visitor would follow a few days later, he felt himself doomed.

So when a fishing trip was proposed by the Larderer to replenish the stores in preparation for the papal visit, Hugh jumped at the chance to

escape from his problems. It was so peaceful sitting out on the Stour
under the shade of the trees with his line dangling in the water. But
all he could think about was the cope. The problem spun around and
around in his mind. All day he sat. He didn't catch a single fish. When
the other brothers packed up their rods and lines and baskets, Hugh
was still sitting there in the twilight, staring into space.

Then he started and looked around, not knowing what had
broken his reverie. He saw a cowled figure in Austin robes walking
towards him from the footbridge to the castle. Hugh frowned.
It was no one he recognised.

The strange friar stopped in front of Hugh and said, 'It's late to be
out fishing. But you look like you have many cares to think about.'

Hugh stared at the man. His cowl covered his face, his sleeves
his hands, and his robe was so long that it covered his feet. Hugh
could hardly tell if there was a man in there at all, but his voice was
most beautiful. So calming, so reassuring …

'Tell me,' said the man, settling down beside him. 'Sometimes
it's easier to unburden yourself to a stranger than to those who
know you…'

Hugh found himself telling the whole sorry story of the
pawning and the luxuries and the cope – and the papal ambassador's impending visit.

To his surprise the man began to laugh. Hugh nearly jumped to his feet in affront, but the man waved him down.

'Don't take offence,' he said. 'I only laugh because once I was in your shoes. It was exactly the same. I was a Sacristan and in the same pickle as you. But I found a solution, and you may find that it suits you too. Would you like to hear it?'

And of course Hugh did.

'As Sacristan, you are presumably in charge of the sale of candles to those who come to your fine chapel to pray?'

Hugh nodded.

'Well then, your way is clear. Mice eat candles; it's the perfect excuse. Stash away your candles and tell the beekeeper that they were eaten. He'll give you a new set. Sell them all, but keep the monies from the old set for yourself; you'll see that the money soon builds up. And when the pilgrims have gone, well, they'll never know if you pinch out their candle and sell it all over again. If you find yourself getting low, just ply the beekeeper with the mouse trick again and he'll give you more. What could be more perfect?'

Hugh had to agree that it was a wonderful plan.

'There is just one thing,' said the stranger. 'The first candle you sell, put it to one side. Keep it safe, for once it burns out I'll come to claim you as my own. I think you understand me.'

With that the figure got to his feet, and disappeared into the gathering dusk.

Hugh jumped up and hurried home. The plan was so perfect in his mind that he hardly gave a thought to the stranger's last comment and what it meant. But he did remember to put aside that first candle on the sill of the sacristy window.

Even within the first couple of days the money flooded in. Emboldened by the new scheme he pawned a number of items to get the cope back. Days later it was presented to the papal ambassador under Prior Wilfred's proud gaze.

For a while, things went well. Hugh slowly began to get things back from the pawnshop. He tried not to go into town, and considered himself a reformed character. But it wasn't to last long. After the papal ambassador's visit, Prior Wilfred was struck with reforming zeal. He started to go through the books to ensure that all was well, and soon discovered that his priory was seething with petty corruption. The Cellarer's accounts were wrong, the Larderer had no control over his provisions, and the Sacristan was using far more candles than he used to. It was time, he decided, to call them to account and impose some order on the house.

Hugh's punishment for the candle scam was onerous to him, but he had to admit it was fitting: a diet of bread and water, and not to leave the priory's precincts for a month. He also had to hand over the keys to the treasure chests and the candle box. Although he recognised the punishment was fair, he chafed against it and watched with envy every mouthful of the other friars' dinners.

One day the Prior announced that he and all the other brothers were going out hunting. All except Hugh. He watched them ride away with a bitter heart. After all, hadn't he been mending his ways? He determined he would do nothing all day in protest. But at dusk, when he heard the returning hunters' horn, he remembered there was one task he had to do: he had promised the Cellarer that he would put out the salt on the refectory table ready for dinner.

He hurried down to the cellar, but realised that it would now be quite dark. He hurried back to the sacristy, then remembered he didn't have the key to the candle box anymore. But he had to find a candle! He scrabbled about, and in the dust on the sacristy window sill he found a solitary candle. Lighting it without a thought, he hurried off.

By the time he reached the cellar his belly was growling, and he couldn't immediately find the salt. He lifted cover after cover. Under one he found a cold larded capon: the Prior's supper. He was so hungry he didn't even think. Before he knew it, all that was left was bones, sucked clean. Then he came to himself. Not knowing what to do he slapped the cover back on the dish. Finally he located the salt and ran upstairs with it, leaving the candle burning all by itself in the cellar.

At eight o'clock Prior Wilfred was presented with his supper. Full of anticipation, he plucked the cover off – and there in front of him was nothing but a pile of bones. He stared at them, hardly able to believe his eyes. Then fury rose in him. It was clear who had done this. Only one friar had been left in the priory that day.

'Brother Hugh, may you go to the Devil for this!'

At that same moment the candle in the cellar guttered and died. And a terrible scream was heard from the refectory stairs.

For a moment everyone in the refectory sat rooted to their seats in terror. Then, as one, they rushed to the stairs, Prior Wilfred at their head.

The stairs were in darkness, but the Prior thought he glimpsed a dark, cowled figure slip out the door towards the buttery. In the air was a terrible smell of sulphur.

He had no time to think about that because there in front of him, sprawled at the foot of the stairs, was Hugh. On his face was an expression of utter terror, he was covered in burns, and his head was dashed to pieces on the steps. Gently, they carried him to the infirmary, but he was dead already. There was nothing to be done except pray for his soul.

On the frater steps was a terrible bloodstain. No matter how much the brothers scrubbed, scraped and sprinkled it with holy water, it wouldn't budge. The friars shook their heads, but Prior Wilfred remembered the dark figure he'd seen and he knew what it meant. The priory had the mark of the Devil. It would never be cleaned away until judgement day.

This story was recorded from an old Clare storyteller in the early years of the twentieth century by Lady Katherine Barker, whose husband owned Clare Priory, and was recorded in her history of the building. The story is a remarkable survival, as it records locations in the priory that were not known at the time of telling. Later excavations demonstrated everything the storyteller said about the layout of the medieval priory to be true. Clare Priory was the first house of the Augustinian, or Austin Friars founded in England in the mid-thirteenth century, but it was dissolved by Henry VIII during the dissolution of the monasteries. The stain on the step was uncovered in the early twentieth century, still as dark as it was when it was made.

TWENTY-TWO

MALEKIN

It was harvest time at Langham, and the whole village was out in the fields. It didn't matter if you were young or old, a man or a woman; if you were fit enough to reap, you worked. The year before, there had been a woman who hadn't taken part: she'd been labouring in a different way. This year she was out with the rest. Her baby daughter had to come too, but she was too heavy to carry, so the mother had left her under the shade of some trees by the edge of the field, swaddled up to keep her from crawling off.

At lunchtime she came back to check and feed her, but she had to leave her again for the afternoon.

That day, the work went on into the sunset, and it was almost dark when the weary workers began to make their way back to the village. The mother heard the baby before she saw her. A thin, high wailing filled the air, not her child's usual lusty cry. She ran across the field and scooped her daughter up in her arms. She jiggled her and hummed to soothe her, but the baby wouldn't stop crying; she wailed all the way home. When she and her husband got in, the man glared at the baby and said he was off to quench his thirst.

The woman watched him go. Then she laid the baby in the cradle and looked at her for the first time since she'd picked her up at the field's edge. This baby who stared back at her was not her own child. Her daughter was plump-cheeked and bonny. This child was thin and sallow. Her daughter had thick golden curls. This child had only a dusting of limp hair. And her daughter's eyes had been full of laughter, but this child looked back her with the saddest, oldest look she'd ever seen.

The woman turned from the cradle. She walked outside until she was sure that no one would see her, then fell to her knees and wept. That wasn't her child, but it was clear what had happened. In the dusk the ferishers had come and taken her babe and left their own unwanted changeling in her place. As her tears dried, anger filled her, and she jumped up and ran back to the house where the baby was still wailing. The child could go! She'd take her and dump her back on the field edge and let God have the care of her if he wished it.

But when she looked into the baby's sad eyes, she stopped. Somewhere a ferisher was rocking her daughter on her knee, smoothing those blond curls and singing strange fairy songs to her. How could she not do the same for the ferisher's child? So she picked the frail little girl up and sang to her all the songs she'd sung to her own child, as the tears rolled down her cheeks.

The next day, she awoke to the changeling's crying, and once more she soothed her. But then she noticed something on the cradle linen. A coin. It was like no coin she'd ever seen, but it was solid silver. She understood. The ferishers were thanking her for taking care of their own.

So the woman of Langham cared for the ferisher infant. The child thrived and grew into a strange little girl full of way-wardness and strange moods. The woman came to love her, but she never stopped wondering what happened to her own babe.

Not ten miles away, in the village of Dagworth, another mother smiled proudly down at her firstborn. A son this time, heir to the Manor of Dagworth. Lady Margaret FitzHarvey loved her little boy with all of her heart.

She watched him grow from a toddling babe to a running, shouting little lad, until he was a boisterous boy of near eight summers. Richard would run off over the watersplash into the village and play with the village lads. Every moment he was gone she would miss him; her only child.

One day, as she was putting a new tunic in his room, she heard something. A girl's voice, high and piping, seemed to be talking to her dolls just as Lady Margaret remembered doing in her own girlhood. But the room was empty. She shook herself and quickly walked away.

But that night, Richard came to her and said, 'Someone's been playing with my soldiers. They're all messed up.'

The servants were questioned, but all swore that they'd not been in the room or touched a thing. Over the next few days, Richard forgot the incident, but Lady Margaret could not get that little voice out of her head. Then other things began to happen.

All the laundry was put away in the wrong places. Richard got his mother's clothes. Lady Margaret had servants' dresses. The laundry maid got a thrashing, but she swore they'd been done right. The next day, a pot boiling on the fire leapt up in the air – when there was no one near it. And that night in the hall all the meat jumped up and hung in the air above the table until someone screamed.

By now, everyone seemed to be hearing that little piping voice. But, it was strange; the priest swore that the child spoke to him in Latin and wanted to argue the scriptures, whereas Lady Margaret knew she'd heard it speaking Norman-French. And the servants all said they'd understood it, and they only spoke English. The voice was even heard singing in the chapel.

It was noticed, too, that food was going missing. The scullery maid got the blame for that at first, but it soon became apparent that food was vanishing from places the maid couldn't get to. It was the spirit, people said, and generally they smiled.

One day, Lady Margaret saw Richard running through the courtyard talking to someone – though there was no one there. She called him over.

'Who was that you were talking to?'

'That's Malekin,' cried the boy. 'She's my best friend. Even though you can't see her, she's got the best ideas. She's wicked!'

Lady Margaret knew then that it had to stop.

She went to the priest and said, 'It is unnatural to have this spirit haunting us. You must exorcise it.'

The priest was reluctant, as it seemed to him that the spirit meant no harm, but Lady Margaret was adamant.

Soon the news was all round the manor. The servants were upset, for they had become fond of the spirit. One of Lady Margaret's maids slipped into Richard's room, went down on her knees and begged the spirit to appear.

'Please, please, show yourself to me and I swear I will not try to touch you. Tell me how you came here and what manner of spirit you are, as you are in great danger.'

The room suddenly dimmed, as if it was twilight and not midday, and there, in the shadows, stood a tiny child. She looked to be no more than a year old and had curly golden hair. She was dressed in a white shift that shimmered in the dim light.

'I don't remember my name, but *they* call me Malekin. I'm from – I think it was it called Langham? I don't remember my mother – not really. *They* took me away. I don't like living with *them*, and I can't eat *their* food, so I come into houses, but people always

chase me away. For seven years I've been living with *them*, but *they* say if I last seven more I can go home.'

The maidservant ran to tell her mistress, and when Lady Margaret heard all this she was touched. A changeling child. She brought out her cradle that had been empty so long, and imagined how it would have been if Richard had been snatched. How could she turn out this other mother's child?

So Malekin stayed in Dagworth Manor. Every day the servants put out a portion of food in a certain place, and by the end of that day it would be gone.

Richard loved his companion, but he was a growing boy. Soon he was fostered away to learn all he needed to know to become a knight, and he soon forgot Malekin. When he came home, nine years later, he was a young man. Everything looked the same but somehow his old home felt empty. Then he remembered the spirit.

He asked his mother about her, and Lady Margaret said that the spirit had departed two or three years before and had not been heard of since. Richard remembered then what his mother's maid had said. Malekin had had seven more years to wait until she was free, so she was gone. Maybe, he thought, she'd gone home to Langham.

So he rode over to Langham to see if there was a young woman there with blond curly hair, new to the village and ... strange. He didn't know what he would do if he found her, but he knew that he had to try. When he came to Langham, the villagers shook their heads. No, there was no one like that, they said. There had been a young woman, a strange, fey creature who loved the wild places and had never seemed quite their own. But she'd grown up in the village. Besides, they said, she'd slipped away into the woods two or three years ago and had not been seen since.

There was nothing to do but ride home. But as he left the village he saw a woman walking with her little curly-haired granddaughter, a blonde moppet of perhaps three or four. The child stopped dead when she saw him, and fixed him with a gaze far more knowing than her tender years. Then she gave him a brilliant, almost coquettish smile and waved. Richard was a polite young man, and he waved back. But as he rode away he shook his head, wondering why he felt he knew a child he'd never seen before.

This story, or part of it, is another tale from Ralph of Coggeshall. The story of the Malekin at Dagworth Manor is not well known. It must be one of the first accounts not only of a human caught in the fairy world but also of poltergeist activity. Revd Hollingsworth recorded the story of the woman of Langham who showed kindness to a fairy child and is rewarded for it. It seemed to me that if it could happen once, then it must have happened many times. It is said, too, that there are hidden tunnels in the castle ditches at Langham. Are they entrances to the fairy world?

TWENTY-THREE

THE MURDER IN THE RED BARN

Maria Marten never had much for herself. At eight she was sent away to be a nursery maid to the vicar at Layham. She quite liked that. But when she was only nine, her mother died. Maria had to come home to be a mother to her younger sister and keep house for her father. She was determined to be a success, and the other villagers gave her admiring looks for her determination, but as she grew and the days rolled by – always the same, year in, year out – she began to feel trapped.

She hardly ever left Polstead. Layham was only a three-mile walk, but it seemed another world now. When her father married again she hoped she might get another position, but it was not to be. More siblings were born, and it was made clear that Maria was needed at home.

Nearly ten years passed and Maria grew into a woman. Her youthful beauty and fresh charm caught the eye of the second son of one of the well-off farming families in the village, the Corders. Thomas was charming and persuasive. At last Maria found something that was for herself, something real. For three years they met in secret. Then the fun ended. Maria wasn't surprised to find that she was pregnant – only that she got away with it for that long.

But when she told her lover, he wasn't kind. He wouldn't marry her. Well, she knew that. She knew she was good for a tumble, but that no rich farmer would marry a mole-catcher's daughter. But he wouldn't acknowledge the child either, or support it in any way.

The months passed slowly. No more admiring looks, just whispers and gossip. Maria couldn't look forward to the child. It was born sickly, and she felt little for it; she just felt more trapped. Sometimes she would sit and weep as the baby cried and cried. Her daughter soon died. Maria wept again, but she felt a knot within her loosen. Perhaps there was a chance she might yet get away.

That year she dressed herself up as finely as she could for the Cherry Fair, and went with her head held high. It worked. She caught the eye of Peter Matthews. He was rich and exciting. Though she knew that a man like that would never marry her, she didn't care. Peter was an escape. He took her to Ipswich, and once he dressed her up in fine clothes and took her to London. It was a dream come true – except she wasn't married.

Then she discovered she was pregnant again. That was the end of the affair, but Peter was happy to acknowledge the child and he sent £5 every month. The baby, called Thomas after her father, thrived. The money coming in every month brought some ease to the Marten family.

But Maria was still restless. As Thomas grew, she felt that old trapped feeling settle on her once more. Then she caught the eye of another Corder.

William was Thomas's younger brother. He was a bright boy and was sent away to school in Hadleigh. He was unpopular there, and now back home people thought there was something odd about him. The last year had been hard. In eighteen months all three of his brothers and his father had died. His amorphous ambitions were dashed. The farm was his, whether he wanted it or not. He chafed against the responsibility. There were rumours of pig stealing, and sightings of him with Hannah Fandango and the notorious 'Beauty' Smith.

Perhaps William and Maria recognised each other's restlessness, and were drawn to each other because of it. For a time they were happy. Hardly a day passed that William didn't come to the Marten house. And, after she had put little Thomas to bed, Maria would put on her shawl and bonnet and slip away into the dusk. She'd take the path from her cottage through the fields, skirt alongside the wood, jump the pond, and then she'd be there. On the hill up Shelley road stood a barn belonging to the Corders, the roof gleaming red in the sunset. There they would meet and stay all night amidst the hay.

The inevitable happened, and Maria was sure that William would turn away from her just as his brother had. But William didn't go. He was attentive throughout her pregnancy, and the word 'marriage' began to be spoken – though after the birth, of course. For now, Maria and her family weren't allowed to say anything in case William's mother caught wind of it.

William was good to Maria. When she started to show, he whisked her away to Sudbury and set her up in rooms with a servant all her own. She went home straight after the birth, but the baby was sickly. When he was only six weeks old, he died in his step-grandmother's arms. Maria's hopes shrivelled, but William didn't leave her.

Things changed. The death of the child stood between them. They argued constantly and sometimes William would look at Maria in a way that chilled her. Then £5 from Peter Matthews went missing. William denied he'd taken it, but Maria was sure he had.

Her parents nagged away at William to make an honest woman of her. At first William was resistant. He cited his mother as a reason. He hardly knew what he wanted himself. But to marry Maria? There was an increasingly desperate look in his eyes, and his fights with Maria intensified. Then, suddenly, he changed his tune. He began to speak of marrying in Ipswich so his mother wouldn't know. Maria allowed herself to hope she might finally escape.

On 18 May 1828 William arrived at the Martens' cottage with a bundle under his arm. He told Maria that he had a licence for them to be married in Ipswich later that day and that she must meet him in the Red Barn at midday. But she must not be seen. He used his mother as an argument, saying she was watching them in case he tried to marry Maria. He opened the bundle, full of clothes that had belonged to his dead brothers.

'Dress as a man and come. I won't wait after midday.'

In high excitement Maria stripped off her gown and pulled on the britches over her petticoat. She kept on her stays – the ones with the ash busk at the front to replace a broken bone. She kept her reticule tied at her waist. The jacket strained over her breasts, but a green scarf hid that. She piled up her hair under the hat, then stuffed the rest of her clothes into the sack. She kissed her son, told him she'd be home soon and then they'd all be a family at last. She said farewell to her stepmother and set off up the path through the fields to the Red Barn. Her new life was about to begin.

That was the last time Maria Marten was seen in Polstead.

William came back a few days later and explained that the wedding had not, in fact, taken place. Maria was in Great Yarmouth with friends of his, and they would wed soon. She had hurt her hand, so hadn't been able to send a letter, but she sent her love and kisses to young Thomas.

William stayed for the hay harvest, working long hours until the Red Barn was full. But he was not himself. One time he turned to a worker and said, 'You should kill me, you know.' The worker just smiled, hoping he was joking. Mrs Stow, who lived nearby, had the strangest conversation with him: she asked if he was worried that Maria might go off with someone else, up in fancy Great Yarmouth.

'No,' he said. 'When I am away, I am sure no one else is with her.'

'Do you think you'll have more children with her?'

Again the answer was no. 'Maria will never be troubled by any more children. She has had her number.'

It left Mrs Stow quite unsettled. She couldn't help but remember that she'd lent her second-best spade to him the day that Maria had gone away.

Autumn came, and William was away to London. He said Maria was with him. Then they were off to the Isle of Wight, and would send for young Thomas as soon as they could. He wrote that Maria was sad that her parents hadn't written: had they not received her last letter?

No letter came, and as the winter drew on, Maria's parents began to worry. On Christmas Eve her stepmother had a dream. She saw Maria dead in the Red Barn. At first she didn't dare say anything, but the dream came again and again. She begged her husband to look. He brushed her fears aside until spring. On 19 April 1829, he and a lad went and dug in the now empty barn. They discovered Maria's poor remains just inches beneath the floor.

It was certainly her. There was the ash busk in her stays, the green neckerchief. It was plain she had been very badly used. So now the search was on for William Corder.

A detective was hired by the authorities. He discovered that William had left a strange trail. He had gone to London, but not to meet Maria. Instead he had advertised for a wife in a newspaper. The replies had flooded in:

'I am a young person without parents.'

'Pardon the warmth of my expressions, please don't think me forward.'

'I have a sweet little girl, who is my greatest comfort.'

'I shall be walking by in a black gown with a scarlet shawl, if you will be there…'

William had met with one of these women and married her. They went to Brentwood in Essex to start a girl's school.

One night William had a dream. He dreamt that he saw his dead brothers and sisters walking past in their shrouds, their eyes burning into him. The next morning, the detective knocked on the door. William protested that he had never known Maria, but he was taken away.

He was taken back to the inquest at Polstead. All the old tales about pig stealing and 'Beauty' Smith were rolled out. Soon William was carried off in irons to Bury gaol.

By now the whole country knew the story. On the day of the trial, Bury's streets were filled with people wanting to catch a glimpse of William Corder. People climbed on roofs to get a better look. The press of people made it difficult for William to get inside. There was a riot when the public weren't allowed in the court room. There, William spun a new tale. Maria had killed herself, he said. No one believed him. The evidence of the body was too strong. No one could do that to themselves.

His wife begged him to clear his soul. The night before he was to die he confessed. The record was straight, even though it did Maria no good. Who can say what good it did William? The next morning he was hanged before an audience of thousands.

He was not buried – murderers' bodies went to science. William's body was taken away and dismembered, his skeleton used for students' anatomy lessons, his skin tanned and his scalp pickled.

For many years, his skeleton stayed in the West Suffolk Hospital in Bury. In the 1870s a Dr Kilner came into possession of the skin and scalp. He decided he wanted the skull as well. By now the skull was in the museum of the hospital, and it was easy for the doctor to stay after hours, sneak into the museum and take the skull. Or so it seemed. As he tried to light his candles to see what he was doing, the last one kept going out. When he finally got it lit, the others went out. But he persevered, muttering about breezes, and carried the skull home.

He installed it in a case in his drawing room. A couple of days later a maid came to his room to say there was a strange man in the drawing room, dressed in strange, old-fashioned clothes. When he went downstairs, there was no one. After that there were several sightings by the women of the house: footsteps heard in the corridors and heavy breathing, muttering and sobbing from the drawing room.

Kilner never heard anything, but he started to dream terrible dreams.

After several sleepless nights, he decided he must get rid of the skull. The next night he heard something. On coming out onto the landing, he saw a white hand hovering over the drawing-room door. He grabbed a brass candlestick for protection and made his way downstairs. When he flung open the door no one was there. There was the skull grinning up at him from its plinth, but the glass case was completely smashed.

He gave the skull to a friend, Mr Hopkins. Hopkins had just bought the governor's house on the old prison site and was delighted to have a souvenir of the prison's most famous inmate. But almost immediately things began to go wrong for Hopkins. He had a bad fall, his horse fell and had to be put down, and lots of other things kept going wrong. The skull had to go. So Hopkins found a gravedigger, and the skull was quietly buried in a village churchyard near Bury. It was said that William Corder was at last at peace.

Fascination with this tale has never ceased. From the beginning people were intrigued. The Red Barn was picked apart. Maria's grave in Polstead was chipped away to nothing by souvenir hunters. There are plays, novels and albums about the tale. My stepfather told me that when his parents moved to Ipswich, the first place his grandfather wanted to go was Polstead because he'd seen a music hall performance of this story. One of my own most memorable school trips was to Moyses Hall in Bury where I saw the book bound in Corder's skin.

TWENTY-FOUR

A STRANGE AND
TERRIBLE WONDER

Hugh Bigod, the old Earl of Norfolk, was desperate. King Henry II had him cornered. Hugh had chanced everything in supporting Henry's son, the Young King, in his rebellion against his father. But he had lost. When St Edmund saw off the rebel forces at Fornham near Bury in 1173, Hugh should have given up. But that wasn't Hugh's way. Instead, he made a deal with the Devil. If he won, he would have power and control over the Young King. If he lost, there would be Hell to pay. So he kept on fighting.

He sacked Norwich, then rode south to secure his castles. No sooner had he ridden south than he heard King Henry was after him once more. Fearing an earthly demise and with the whiff of sulphur in the air, Hugh fled. Through Ipswich, then Ufford. At first he thought Framlingham Castle would be safe, but the King's men cut off him off from his route. His only hope was to get to the castle at Bungay before the soldiers caught him up. Past Saxmundham he rode, muttering to himself, 'If only I was in my castle at Bungay, I would not set a button by the King of Cockney.'

The King's men were always behind him. But Hugh's horse was fleet, and he was on his home ground. He shot up the Earlsway past the boundary oak at Bramfield. He fled right through the centre of Halesworth. Then he was on the Bungay road, racing past the leafy pilgrims' rest at Illketshall. Bungay was in sight. But Bungay wasn't as safe as it seemed.

King Henry marched on Bungay, and his men started to undermine the foundations of Hugh's castle. Hugh knew he was defeated. He was forced to surrender everything. Hell awaited. But he had no choice. He paid a thousand marks to the King and kept his castles – but he knew it would take more than money to keep his soul.

Hugh was never one to give in to a problem. All he knew was fighting. He set out for the Holy Land to fight, to cleanse his soul of the Devil's taint. It was one fight too many for his weary old body. He died in 1176, eighty-one years old.

The Devil was there to greet him at the fiery gates to Hell.

'Welcome, Hugh,' he cried. 'I've been waiting for you! I'm touched at how you've tried to redeem yourself, so I'll make you another bargain. You need more redemption. If your spirit can redeem itself back home in Suffolk, then I'll to let you go up to the Other Place.'

Hugh knew he'd be foolish to refuse, so he opted to become a restless spirit. But he should have realised that the Devil is canny. A spirit he became, but not a thinking, reasoning, human spirit. Hugh was transformed into a great black dog with a shaggy coat and burning red eyes. Worse than that, he had no memory of who he was and what he had to do; only a burning anger that as a dog he couldn't understand. He only knew he had to get home.

Once more he raced across towards Bungay, but it took longer than he expected. Bungay was different. His castle wasn't the same. It had new, strong walls, but inside he could see his keep. It called to him, and he slipped inside. He paced through it, searching for … something. A child dressed in strange clothes appeared from a staircase. He growled. The child screamed and fled, telling everyone he'd seen a black dog as big as a calf. The shock was so great that the boy died a week later. This was not the kind of deed the Devil wanted. Deep inside, the black dog knew it, and he grew even angrier.

The legend of Black Shuck, the shaggy dog of Suffolk, was born. He haunted Bungay. He was seen in the castle and the priory grounds. He roamed the lanes all around. If you saw him, it was said, you or someone you loved would die.

On 4 August 1577, Black Shuck's fury reached boiling point. Everything was different and kept changing! His castle was a ruin and he had centuries of misery locked inside himself. It had to come out.

It was a hot day, even by nine that morning. The rector began the sermon, but as he spoke the church grew darker and darker. The congregation began to shift uneasily, hearing rumbles of thunder in the distance. Just as the rector began the second lesson, there was a brilliant flash of light and a crack of thunder so loud that someone screamed.

The rain came, hammering so hard on the roof that it almost drowned out the thunder. The storm raged round and round the church. No one knew what to do.

'Everyone, stay in your seats!' cried the rector. 'This is God's house. He will protect us!'

As soon as he spoke there was another brilliant flash and a deafening crack. The air suddenly seemed thick and treacly. With sudden horror the congregation realised they were no longer alone in the church.

Standing in the central aisle was a huge black dog. The congregation stared, transfixed. With another flash of light, the dog bounded up the aisle towards them, hackles raised and growling.

People fell to their knees.

'Lord God, protect us from this devil.'

'Please, God, make it go away.'

With a flick of his tail Shuck whipped a man. He dropped like a stone. The dog spun around and crashed into another man, and he too fell.

Panic ripped through the church. Everyone surged to their feet, scrambling over each in their desperation to get out, get away and escape this awful fiend.

'Stop, stop!' cried the rector.

The Shuck was everywhere, snarling, growling, his burning eyes glittering in the dark church as he leapt from pew to pew, batting out at people as they tried to flee. One man he knocked down shrivelled under his touch like a piece of leather caught in a fire.

'We must pray for God's mercy!' The rector's cry echoed over the screams. Everyone dropped to their knees.

The Shuck gave a shriek, turned and raced to the north door. Everyone watched as he scraped desperately at the wood until the door gave away and the dog raced out.

The congregation stayed on their knees as the church slowly brightened, not daring to stop praying in case the Shuck came back. After a long while the rector got to his feet, and slowly the rest of the congregation followed suit. Numbly they stared around. The rector came down and moved among them, patting a shoulder here, an arm there. The two men first touched by the Shuck were dead, terror imprinted on their faces. The third man still lived, but his shrivelled side was limp, all life gone from it. On the north door were the smoking scratch marks the Shuck had left behind.

The storm was still moving, heading south and east to Blythburgh, where the villagers were all in church for the morning service.

Lightning struck the tower. There on the rood-beam stood the Shuck. He leapt down and raced through the church, claws skittering on the tiled floor. He knocked two men down dead as he went. A boy broke loose of his mother's grip and fled. Shuck had him too, and burnt his brother as he tried to pull the younger boy away.

The dog raced up the aisle to the north door and once more he scrabbled until he could burst free. While the people of

Blythburgh stood in shock, the storm moved away down the Blyth and out to sea.

The Shuck was known everywhere in East Anglia, but it seemed that some of his anger had drained away with those vicious attacks. Those who saw him afterwards on the lonely lanes said the dog hardly noticed them. It was as if he was in another reality and didn't register the mortal world at all.

Trapped inside the Shuck, Hugh battled to resurface and begin his quest for redemption. For many years he tried. By the nineteenth century the old dog seemed to be learning new tricks.

In 1842 a group of women were gathering reeds for their roofs near Catfield Hall. They were trespassing, so had to work in the dead of night. Suddenly, they saw a man coming towards them in the moonlight.

'The keeper!'

As they turned to flee, a huge black dog appeared among them. It raced away, then turned and raced back again. The women froze rigid with fear until one said, 'Do you think he wants us to follow him?'

The dog led them along a safe path through the marsh. Once back on dry land, the women ran and the dog ran beside them. When they finally dared stop running, they found that the dog had gone.

Twenty years later, a young woman was hurrying home alone after dark. As she walked past a shadowy lane, two men jumped out in front of her. She felt sure they were about to attack her. Then, from out of nowhere, a huge black dog appeared, growling at the men. They legged it fast away, and the woman ran too – and didn't stop or look behind her until she was safe home.

In the early years of the twentieth century a man was cycling home after a darts match, when through the darkness he saw a great black dog sitting by the signpost to his village. It didn't move, so he inched past, his neck prickling as he went by. As he cycled, he heard the dog racing behind him, getting closer by the moment. His nose filled with its rank smell as it passed him; then it wheeled around and stopped in the middle of the road, growling at him.

The man dismounted and backed away, and just as he got to the side of the road a motorcar came by at speed, without any lights on. It crashed into the dog, knocked the man further into the ditch, then drove off even faster. The man picked himself up and clambered back to the road. He expected to see a dead dog. But the dog was still sitting there, as large as life. Then it stood, turned, and vanished, leaving him alone on the empty road. The man realised that the dog had saved his life.

Night by night, Hugh is coming back to himself. He is redeeming himself, one good deed at a time. One day, perhaps, Black Shuck will no longer haunt East Anglia, when Hugh Bigod has finally gained his immortal prize.

Hugh Bigod is painted as a blackguard in East Anglia, but in truth he was no better or worse than many nobles of his day. King Henry II came to power after a long civil war in England, one in which Hugh was on the other side. In the twelfth century, nobles had great power, and by making alliances, had the potential to overthrow regimes. Hugh was one of many who rose against Henry. He was a powerful man in East Anglia, owning the castles of Bungay, Framlingham and Walton near Felixstowe, and he was not afraid to go after what he wanted.

TWENTY-FIVE

THE LEGEND OF
THE HOLY WELL

The year was 1010, and East Anglia was at war again. Six years before, Ulfketel the Bold, war leader of the East Anglians, had sent Sweyn Forkbeard and his Danes home across the North Sea after the burning of Thetford and Norwich. Now they were back, with the feared Jomsvikinga warriors at their side. They landed near Ipswich, and the people wept in fear that their town would soon be burned. The Danes were eager to meet Ulfketel in battle and went south to Nacton where the East Anglians waited.

Many died that Ascension Day, on the heathlands north of the river, among the oak and the birch and the pine. Thorkell the Tall led the Jomsvikinga. They knew no fear, and they cut down the flower of the English without a qualm. But the East Anglians held firm until Thorkytel Mare's Head fled. After that, it was a rout, and the English dead lay bleeding on the thirsty earth.

One group of Jomsvikinga was cut off from the rest. When the East Anglians found them, they fell on them with all the force of their fear and anger and cut them down until the heather bloomed scarlet. Only a man and a boy still stood, the man trying to be everywhere against the English warriors to protect the lad. But it was too much. Again and again their swords pierced him until he could barely lift his sword. The boy leapt forward, his sword held high in both hands.

'You leave Hurder alone!'

Then there was a sharp pain in the lad's head and he knew no more.

When he awoke it was dark. For a long moment he just lay there, hardly knowing even who he was, let alone where. Only knowing that his head hurt. Then it all came flooding back: the battle, his father, the blow to the head. Slowly, he eased himself up and looked around. A full moon hung overhead, and he could see clearly that he lay among the dead. The ravens had begun their busy work. Not far off, he heard the howl of a wolf.

He had to find Hurder, at least give him a decent burial. He was the only father the boy could remember. He searched through the bodies of his fallen comrades, his heart bleeding. At last he found what he was looking for. Hurder was cut and wounded in so many places. He looked dead, but when the boy pressed his ear to Hurder's chest he heard a faint thumping.

'Hurder! Father!' he cried, and the older man's eyes opened.

'Praise Odin,' Hurder whispered. 'He lives! I knew I was right to knock him down.'

'Hurder, we must get out of here. If the English find us tomorrow when they come to claim their dead, then we will be killed for certain.'

Hurder shook his head.

'You go, Ivan. I'm too far gone. Go to Ipswich. If the city is burning, then we've had the victory and Thorkell will be there. He'll protect you, lad.'

But Ivan wouldn't leave Hurder behind.

'No! We'll go together.'

He bound the older man's wounds and managed to get him up. They set out towards the town across the dry heathland. Ivan was desperate with thirst. He knew that Hurder must be desperate too; he heard it in his father's rasping breath. But up on the heathland there was only heather and sandy soil, and a few pine and birch trees tall on the horizon.

At last they came to a point where they could see down to the great sluggish stream of the Orwell and, beyond, a red glow rising up over the wooden towers of Ipswich.

'See, Hurder, it's as you said. Thorkell has the victory! Soon we'll be safe.'

But Hurder sagged in his arms and said nothing.

Ivan was determined. He hauled the man up again and half pulled, half dragged him on. He hardly thought of getting to Ipswich, or about the hostile English, but only about water. The more he thought on that, the heavier Hurder became and the drier his own mouth.

Now he was off the heath and into the dark woods near the town. At last he heard the sound of running water and, immediately following that, the tolling of a church bell. He looked around, but all he could see were dark trees and hills. No sign of a village. No sign of a stream.

But the sound he'd heard gave him hope. 'It won't be long now, Hurder; not long.'

Ahead rose a small hill, and on the slope was a little hut of rough-hewn wood. To Ivan it was a palace. With the last of his strength he pulled Hurder forward until they were in front of the hut, then laid him down as gently as he could. He knocked on the door, but there was no answer. He looked inside, but there was no one to be seen in the darkness. Deserted. At that his strength gave out and he collapsed in the doorway.

On the top of the hill under the chestnut trees knelt the owner of the hut. A hermit, praying for the souls lost in the battle and in burning Ipswich. Towards dawn he came down from the hill, and there in front of his hut lay two wounded men, both dressed in Danish clothes. Memories rose. Smoke. Fire. Screaming. The laughter of cruel men. For a moment he wanted to turn away, but he knew that that would not be a Christian act.

So he fetched water from the well and started to clean the men's wounds. Soon he saw that the younger was hardly more than a boy, and there was something about his face that made the hermit sit back on his heels and stare.

Ivan opened his eyes to see a priest staring down at him. He started up and saw to his horror that Hurder lay still.

'Is he–?'

The hermit shook his head.

Hurder's eyes opened. He stared up at the hermit hopelessly, and the hermit saw that the man was not long for this world. But he had to try. He took a scoop of water from the bucket and offered it to him.

'Drink this blessed water, and God will heal you as once he did me.'

But Hurder turned his face away. 'One-eyed Odin is my saviour – your God won't heal me. Let me die seeing that my boy Ivan is safe. He was baptised a Christian – the water will work on him.'

Ivan and the hermit spoke at the same time.

'Hurder, I am safe.'

'How can *your* son be a Christian?'

A faint smile ghosted across Hurder's face.

'He's not my son. When he was a babe, me and my men came a-viking to Felixstowe and I saw his mother and fancied her warming my bed. Didn't see she had a child in her arms until I had her on the boat. I tore him from her, but she was quick. She leapt from my grasp, flung herself in the water and was gone. I was ready to fling the boy in after her, but then he cried and I found I couldn't do it. So I vowed I would raise him as my son, and I made him remember his Christianity in memory of his brave mother.'

He fumbled at his throat, and with trembling hands tugged free a pouch. From the pouch rolled a gold crucifix, enamelled in bright jewel colours.

'This was around his neck. I give it to him now.'

His secret told, the fight went from Hurder and he died.

Ivan flung himself on Hurder, weeping, while the hermit picked up the crucifix with shaking hands and stared at it.

'I know this jewel,' he said to Ivan. 'I put it around your neck the day you were born. You were only a year old when the Vikings came. They took your mother, and when I tried to stop them they beat me until I could hardly stand. I watched her carried out to sea. I saw her leap. I saw him raise you up to throw you in after, and I could no longer watch. I turned and ran, with only my tears as my strength. I ran and ran, but I couldn't escape from what I had seen. My wife, my son. I ran until I had no more

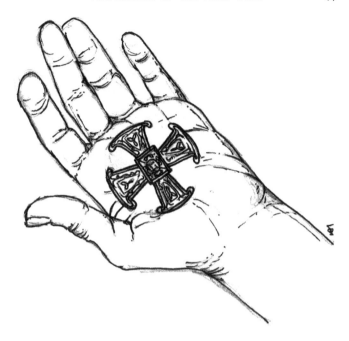

strength and I was desperate with thirst. In this wooded place I fell, and God in his wisdom opened this spring so that I could drink of its sweet waters. I knew then that I was to dedicate my life to God and to his holy spring. I understand now that there was another reason – to bring you to me. Your mother and I – we named you Sigebert. Will you stay with me now, my son?'

They buried Hurder under the chestnut trees on the top of the hill. When that was done, Ivan agreed to stay with his new-found father. Together, they tended the holy spring and praised God. They built a little chapel for the faithful who came to pray. But sometimes Ivan would go to the top of the hill, kneel by Hurder's grave and remember his life as a warrior.

When the hermit died, Ivan stayed on alone. Ipswich was close, but by now it held no attraction to him. Travellers passed by each day, and Ivan gave them sweet water from the well. Eventually people came to the well for healing. By the end of his life, the shrine was flourishing. But Ivan had no successor. When he knew his days were done, he trudged to the top of the hill and lay down beside his two fathers, and the well was left to fall into disrepair.

These hermits were almost forgotten, but the sweet water was not. This area of Ipswich is still called Holywells, and the hill is part of the park there. In the Middle Ages, it was owned by the Bishop of Norwich. If he knew of the wells, he never said. But from 1689, the Cobbold family started using the sweet water to brew beer. They liked the area so much that they bought it, and made it their home. On one side of the park is the hill from which the clear springs ran. This story was written down as a poem by Mrs J. Cobbold and features in Revd James Ford's The Suffolk Garland.

TWENTY-SIX

SYLEHAM LAMPS

You wouldn't have expected a gentle, pragmatic fellow like Fred Warn to be superstitious. But if he was challenged, he would declare that it was certainly true that there were lantern lads out on the marshes – aye, and ghosts too. He was a carter by trade, living up at Shotland Heath by the Waveney, but he did most of his work for Farmer Cossey upriver at Syleham. Cossey liked Fred, and the offer was always there to stop over, but Fred preferred to go home and check up on his old mum.

Fred had reason to know about the lantern lads. The fastest way home was to walk across the marshes, so that's what Fred did. He'd often have a drink with Cossey, though, and always ensured his faithful Suffolk Punch was groomed and fed before he left her in Cossey's stables, as he didn't entirely trust the two lads there to see her right. Then he would take his good, bright lantern and set out home.

A man had to know the paths to get safe across the marshes. It was easy to end up in the marsh. Some parts were drained for cattle, but even those were boggy enough. The rest were a shifting mass of reeds with paths through them. Fred knew the paths well. He'd say he could walk them in his sleep. In truth, though, he often had help.

The first time he'd done the walk, all he could think about were the stories he'd heard as a lad. Stories of lights bobbing out on the marshes, and cries of help that lured men off the paths to their doom. The lantern lads were so common there that people called them 'Syleham lamps'. And those lured by the spirits to their doom didn't rest easy, either. Ghosts were said to walk the marshes in search of the paths they'd lost.

That first walk, Fred saw the glowing orbs floating above the reeds. He told himself he wouldn't be afraid. Instead of responding to the cries, he waved his hand and called, 'Goodnight!' The lamps bobbed closer, and Fred sensed they liked a friendly greeting. And when the silent pale form of a man rose out of the marsh and glided towards him, Fred cried, 'Stick with me, bor, and you'll keep to the path.'

After that, Fred often had a retinue escorting him home, the lamps bobbing alongside and a ghostly presence behind. He never spoke of what he saw, but if anyone said they didn't believe, Fred would quietly say they were wrong.

The two stable lads at Cossey's farm didn't think much of Fred. They hated how the farmer would invite Fred in for a drink, when all they got from him were reprimands for laziness. They hated how Fred groomed his horse himself, as if he didn't trust them. They thought him a bit simple, too, with his belief in the lantern lads. But it was those spirits that gave them the idea.

'We'll teach him a lesson he won't forget,' said the elder.

'We'll get him lost in the marsh,' said the young one.

The very next moonless night they put their plan into action. The elder boy slipped into the farmhouse and took Farmer Cossey's big, bright lamp off its hook. The younger took the stable rush-light down from the wall. Then they set out, as quiet as quiet can be, towards the marshes. They walked along the bank for a while, and then eased themselves down among the reeds to wait.

Just before midnight they heard Fred's tuneless whistling and saw his lamp bobbing towards them on the bank. The elder boy gave the younger a nudge. The younger lofted his dim rush-light and waded out a little way into the marsh. He called out, 'Help!' in a mournful voice, just as if he were a man in trouble – or a luring lantern lad.

He could see Fred's light bobbing along the bank, and hidden in the reeds, the farmer's lamp illuminating his friend, who gestured to him to go out further. So the younger lad edged out a bit more, and the water sloshed over his boots.

'Help!' he cried.

And then, not far behind him, he heard another voice – deeper, louder – cry out.

'Help! Help help!'

When he turned, he saw a light further out on the marshes.

'That's Fred!' he hissed back to his comrade. 'He's in the soup already!'

The older boy bounded through the bog towards his friend, and they splashed off together after Fred, waving their lanterns and laughing. The light bobbed ahead of them, leading them further and further out, into water up to their knees. Still they followed as the lamp beckoned them on, bobbing just out of reach. Then, as they got close, the light flared bright, and they caught a glimpse of a glowing face before the light grew so bright it blinded them. Then it blinked out. Farmer Cossey's lamp slipped out of the elder boy's hands and fell into the water. Darkness surrounded them, save for the dim rush-light. In terror, both the boys floundered, then slipped and plunged into deep water.

Only the dim rush-light still shone. It shook in the younger boy's hand and he had to hold it up high as he was in up to his shoulders. There were things brushing past him in the water.

'Help!' he cried in a much squeakier voice than before. 'Oh, help, please!'

As if conjured by the words, lamps came bobbing out of the darkness. Was it Fred come back to rescue them? No – all around were lamps, and cries of 'Help, help!' in many, many different voices. They were surrounded by Syleham lamps. The boys tried to run, but the water was too deep. Then, right ahead, rising up out of the water was a white shape with two great dark holes for eyes, its arms stretching out to them. Their cries stopped in their throats.

Then they heard Fred's voice calling out to them, but they were too afraid to speak as the lamps bobbed closer. At last the younger boy got so cold that he began to whimper for his mother. Soon they heard Fred splashing through the water and saw his real lantern coming towards them. The Syleham lamps drew back, and there was Fred, real and alive and grinning down at them.

He whistled, and through the water Farmer Cossey's two spaniels came swimming. Half swimming, half wading, the boys clung to the dogs as Fred helped haul them out onto the bank. He gave a command and the dogs raced off home.

The boys stammered out their thanks. Fred shook his head. 'You get back home now – and get that rush-light back on its hook afore you get a beating.'

He turned and set off home. The two shivering boys watched him go. After a while they saw the Syleham lamps rise out of the marshes again. They watched in wonder as they surrounded Fred with light to lead him home.

They were left with just the sputtering rush-light, which was so dim now they could hardly see the path ahead as they trudged home. They never doubted the Syleham lamps again, or begrudged Fred his drink with Farmer Cossey. They knew that when they got back they'd get a bollocking – or worse – for losing the farmer's lamp, but they were so cold and wet and frightened that they didn't rightly care.

This story was recorded by Ruth Tongue at a scout camp in 1928. Will-o'-the-wisps were believed to haunt all the marshy areas of Suffolk, luring travellers to their doom. It was believed, too, that if you got close to one with your lamp the lantern lad would be so angry it would smash it. The Syleham lamps were first recorded in the sixteenth century by William Camden in his Britannia. He says, 'in the low grounds at Sylham, just by Wingfield, are … Sylham lamps, the terror and destruction of travellers, and even of the inhabitants, who are frequently misled by them'.

TWENTY-SEVEN

MAUDE
CAREW

Maude Carew's life had been a great disappointment to her. All her hopes had turned to dust, and now she was mired up in a nunnery with no hope of a happy future. It was all her own fault, she knew. If only she had been prettier, more intelligent, richer, then things would have been very different.

Her woe began three years before in 1444, when she was fifteen and living a quiet life in Bury. Her father, Sir William, was invited to take part in the deputation to King René of Naples to woo his daughter Margaret on behalf of King Henry VI. It was a chance for his youngest child to be seen by the great and the good, so he took Maude with him. Maude loved the pomp and finery of the court of Anjou and soon became friends with Margaret herself. Her father beamed with pleasure, imagining a fine match for a daughter who was friends with a future queen of England.

Her father was delighted to discover there was another Suffolk man at the court, Roger Drury of Rougham. Roger was not young, but he was slim and dark and, to Maude's eye, handsome and perfect in every way. He was travelling Europe to speak with learned men, but there was suspicion of him at the court. It was said that simply with his brooding gaze he could persuade anyone to do anything, and the potions and dusty tomes in his rooms led people to suspect him to be a sorcerer.

He needed no sorcery with Maude. She was fascinated with him, and it seemed to her that he enjoyed her company when she visited him with her father. She began to dream of being Drury's wife, travelling Europe with him on his quest for knowledge. But when she confided her attachment to her father, he frowned.

'He would be a worthy husband, and the Drurys are a fine family – but, my child, you must not get your hopes up. I fear he has little interest in marriage.'

Maude begged her father to talk to him. Because he loved her, Sir William relented. But he came back with a sad face.

'You must put him from your mind. He likes you and spoke warmly of you, child – but that is how he sees you: a pretty child. And don't console yourself that you will be a-growing. He is considering entering a monastery.'

Maude was mortified, and wept all the way home to Bury. When Margaret of Anjou was married to King Henry the following year, she refused to attend. Her father despaired. But while he was away she wrote a letter to her love and sent it to his brother, Sir William, at Rougham.

For a long year she waited for a reply, until at last a letter was delivered.

> To Maude Carew by my hand, Sir William Drury. My brother is no concern of yours, and nor shall he ever be. He has taken holy orders at St Edmund's Abbey in Bury. Ask your father to find you a suitable match, as it is clear that you are in need of a husband's controlling hand. Be thankful that I do not address this to your father, who would mourn that his youngest is so forward.

She hardly took in the rebuke. Her beloved had entered a monastery. Her heart was broken, and she begged her father to let her become a nun. Sir William loved his daughter and knew she wasn't suited to a nunnery; but he couldn't bear her sorrow, so he agreed, hoping she might take solace in God and her holy sisters. She went to a house established in Bury near the hospital of St Saviour's on the road to Fornham. But even there she was not happy. She realised, too late, that she was less likely to catch a glimpse of her love at the Abbey while mired in a nunnery than as a free woman.

So when she learned that the nuns were to be allowed out to see the procession of the King and Queen through the town for the assembly and trial of the Duke of Gloucester, which was to take place there on 10 February that year of 1447, she was happy to think that she would see the outside world – and maybe catch a glimpse of her old friend Queen Margaret and maybe, just maybe, Roger Drury.

It was a cold, clear day, and Maude watched the procession with a jealous pang. Once she had been part of the pomp and ceremony. She had worn fine clothes and jewels. And she had thrown it all away! As Queen Margaret approached, Maude saw her eyes widen, and saw how her friend's gaze lingered on her as she passed by. Maude began to dream of escape. Surely Margaret would help her! Back in the nunnery she quickly penned a letter and sent it to the Queen.

On 23 February, a messenger came to the nunnery to ask that Maude be brought before the Queen. She was allowed to go, and walked towards the abbey with a fast-beating heart. As she and the messenger passed through the great gateway into the abbey grounds, her heart nearly burst from her chest, for there, walking beside the church, was Roger. He didn't notice her, but when he was gone she whispered to the messenger, 'Who was that?'

She was astonished to see him make the sign of the cross.

'That was Father Bernard,' he said, and would say no more.

Queen Margaret welcomed Maude with open arms. 'Here we are, together again at last,' she cried. 'I looked for you at my coronation, but I had no idea that you had taken the veil. How can that be?'

Maude couldn't bear to answer, not with Roger walking around so close. So she asked Margaret about being the Queen.

Margaret seemed glad to answer. 'It would be perfect if it were not for that snake in the grass, the Duke of Gloucester. He is an evil man – a fearful threat to my beloved Henry!'

Maude knew nothing of politics, but even she had heard of Humphrey, Duke of Gloucester. Once regent for King Henry, he was most famous these days for the arrest of his wife for sorcery.

'Yes, he is against all sorcery,' said the Queen. 'And has vowed to seek out all who practise the dark arts. He has a list – and on it I saw a name that you will recognise: Roger Drury, or rather, Father Bernard of this very abbey. Were you not fond of him once?'

Maude was horrified. This Duke was a threat to her beloved? And was an enemy of her friend and the King?

'If he escapes this charge of treason,' Margaret went on, 'he will put to death all on his list. And he is sure to be released. He has bribed and cheated his way into his juror's hearts, and my husband still holds him dear as his uncle. Something must be done; else all that you and I hold dear will be destroyed!'

'But what can be done?' cried Maude.

Queen Margaret smiled, and linked her arm in Maude's.

'That's where you come in, my dear friend. Come into my chamber, and my advisor Cardinal Beaufort will tell you what must be done to save us all.'

That night Maude crept to the chapel of her nunnery and knelt at the altar to pray with gloved hands. Her heart was full of confusion, but Cardinal Beaufort's words had persuaded her that this was the only way. The Cardinal had told her that she was ideally placed to do the deed, thanks to the tunnel between the nunnery and St Saviour's. Tonight, she would slip down the tunnel, go into the Duke's chamber and poison him.

'It is a cunning poison,' the Cardinal had said. 'No one will be able to trace it. It has no smell, no colour. But it is potent – one drop on his face will be enough to kill! But mind you do not get it on yourself, as it would surely kill you as well. It will seep through the thickest fabric…'

Maude did not care about dying. Her life was nothing, and by this deed she would save her beloved Roger. But to take a life to do that? She hardened her heart. Margaret had told her that the Duke was a bad man, so it must be true.

She went to the hidden door behind the altar and down the steps. The air down there was dank and old, but with her candle lighting the way it was a short walk to St Saviour's. As she went, she was aware of other tunnels leading away into darkness, but she ignored them. Her own way was clear. She went up the steps and opened the door. As promised, she was in the Duke's chambers. She went over to the bed where he slept peacefully. He was still a handsome man, despite his years, and didn't look evil at all. Maude took a deep breath and then dripped a drop from the vial onto his face. She watched as his breathing slowed, then stopped, and then she quickly turned away and went back into the tunnel.

As soon as she was the other side of the door she began to shake. As she went down the steps, her shaking grew so great that her lamp went out and she was plunged into blackness. She stumbled down the rest of the steps, and as she did, the vial cracked and she felt a splash on her gloved hands. At once her heart stilled and she remembered the Cardinal's words. Quickly, she tugged off the gloves, even though she knew it would do no good.

She was doomed, but at least she had saved Roger.

Maude knew she mustn't be found in the passages. She did not want to shame her prioress with her evil deed, and so she felt along the walls, trying to find the right passage. On and on she went, with no idea where she was going, and starting to feel light-headed with fear.

Then, up ahead, she saw a light. She called out. The light came towards her, and the last thing she saw before she lost consciousness was a dark face looking down at her.

She awoke in a monk's cell, and sitting across from her was, to her shock, Father Bernard. Her own Roger.

'What have you done?' he cried. 'I found that vial – and a deadlier poison I have rarely seen. You will be dead within an hour, and the bells already toll for your victim! God knows you must be a devil in the robes of a nun.'

Maude shrank back at his words.

'But – I did it for you,' she cried.

Father Bernard looked aghast.

'For me? How can that be? Who are you?'

'Don't you recognise me? I'm Maude Carew–'

'That sweet child turned a murderer? I cannot believe it.'

Her heart fluttered. He still thought her a sweet child. Surely if he heard her history he would understand. So she told him of the Cardinal and the Queen and the list of sorcerers. But he just gave a harsh laugh.

'You are a poor fool, aren't you? You have been tricked, and used, and have damned yourself with murder. God will never receive you now – you will never leave this place, but will haunt it long after it has crumbled into dust. Every night you will pass the sleeping innocents who will dwell here after we are gone and wish that you could sleep, but you never will. How I pity you, you poor, misguided creature.'

But he took her in his arms and held her as she weakened. She wept into his rough habit and felt his tears on her hair. As she slipped away into death, she forgot what she had done, and her last thought was of deep happiness that at last she was enclosed in Roger's loving arms.

When she was dead, Father Bernard carried her back through the tunnels all the way from the abbey to her nunnery and quietly left her in the chapel. In the morning she was found by her fellow nuns, but in the excitement caused by the death of the Duke, the loss of one young nun went unnoticed.

After a time Maude awoke from her deathly sleep into a shadow world. Silently she watched as the War of the Roses began, watched as the Tudors came to the throne and Henry VIII tore down the abbey. She saw the Stuarts, the Georgians, the Victorians, and everyone after. She glided through the ruins, lost and afraid and unable to touch the living who still lived in the houses built into the remains of abbey's west front. Sometimes she would hover over the sleeping householders, in an agony of longing without truly understanding for what she longed.

And every year, in the early hours of the morning of 24 February, she would come into the graveyard by the abbey, and there would be the spirit of her old love, Father Bernard. Yet however much she yearned for him, even in death she could not get near him. He seemed not to notice her as he too paced the graveyard. Still today

she walks the streets of Bury, hoping against hope that one year he will see her and forgive her, and that she will be released from this earthly torment and taken up to heaven.

This story is based on the mystery surrounding the death of Humphrey, Duke of Gloucester. It was originally composed by Margaretta Greene, of the brewing family, who lived in one of the houses in the west front which Maude haunts. Greene's book, The Secret Disclosed *(1861), was a sensation. On 24 February the following year, people turned up to see the ghost, and rioted when she did not appear. But Maude has appeared all over the town as Bury's very own Grey Lady; a fictional ghost who has gained a life of her own.*

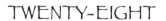

TWENTY-EIGHT

THE WILDMAN
OF ORFORD

Both Eric Ling and Osmer Hart agreed that the sea was the only place to be that day, to get away from the banging and hammering and shouting on the castle building site. Orford had been a sleepy place before Henry II had decided he needed a castle on the coast, and Eric and Osmer were still not used to having their peace disturbed by this relentless Norman activity. Even out at sea, they could see the brooding bulk of the keep rising above the dark forests that clung to the coast. But life went on, and the fish were out there waiting to be brought in, and it had to be said that life was better now that they had the Normans to sell their fish to.

The fishermen rowed out, enjoying the warmth of the dawn sun, but the further out they rowed, the more the sun faded. Then a chill mist came down around them. The whole world faded away so that it was just the two of them, their boat and the slap of the waves against the hull.

'Best row for shore,' said Eric, and they turned the boat about and rowed. The waves swelled and the boat rocked, casting them up and down with greater and greater force, even though there was no wind.

'We've gone the wrong way!' cried Osmer. 'Stupid fog has dragged us out into the deep water!'

For a while they sat there with the boat rocking under them. They could feel the depths beneath in the boat's heavy motion.

'Let's see what fish swim in *these* waters,' said Eric.

Together, they cast out the net and then settled down to wait in the silent mirk.

When they came to haul the net in, they found it heavy.

'We'll come out here again!' cried Eric.

'If we can find "here",' muttered Osmer.

But as the net came up, they saw that their haul appeared to be a mat of seaweed with a few desperate flapping fish caught in it. The two men shook their heads and were about to cast the net back when they saw something move in the mass. As one, they hauled the whole lot into the boat. Slowly, tentatively, they pulled the net back and stared at the green heap in front of them.

'What is it?' breathed Osmer.

They thought of all the tales they knew of the serpents that lived under the sea, and the white horses that would bear you off over the waves, never to return. But this was just a clump of seaweed. With shaking hands, they started to push the weed aside.

As they unpeeled it, Eric gave a shout and the two of them lurched back. For there, lying in the boat before them, was a man. For a moment, they thought they had hauled in a corpse, but then they saw the man's chest rise and fall, and knew it was a far stranger thing that they had caught from the deep.

The man was formed just like any other, but he was covered in hair. He had a thick head of it, a full beard, and coils of hair on his chest and all down his legs. And it was strange hair, thick and heavy, more like pine needles than hair. As they looked closer, they saw gill-slits on his neck, closed now while he breathed the salty air.

Truly, he was not a creature of their world.

'What should we do?' asked Osmer.

Eric stared at the man from the sea for a long while, as the mist began to shred around them. Then he said, 'There's more profit here than a whole year of fishing.'

Osmer nodded and, after another long pause, said, 'It'd be a shame to cast such a heathen down to hell without offering him a chance of salvation.'

By now the mist had lifted. They could see, far in the distance, the tall castle keep marking their home on the coast. Quickly, before he woke up, they wrapped the man in the nets again and tied him up tight. Then they rowed home.

The creature didn't even wake when they bundled him out of the boat and carried him up towards the castle, ignoring all the calls and the questions. They caused such a stir that it was the Constable himself, Bartholomew de Glanville, who came down to meet them.

Eric and Osmer told their tale – the sea mist, the boat rowed far out to sea, the heavy net … and the man. De Glanville stared with a dispassionate eye at the unconscious figure tied up in the nets, then he gestured to a clerk, and a bag of coins was thrown to the fishermen. Two guards stepped forward.

'Take the thing to the dungeon and chain it,' said de Glanville.

The man from the sea awoke to the press of cold stone all around him, his limbs heavy in the thick air and the darkness, and with strange links of cold, hard stuff on his wrists and at his ankles. The last thing he remembered was the squirming ropes cast towards him as he floated under the waves, straining to catch a little of the day's warmth. Here, he could hardly smell the sea – only the reek of filth and meat and damp earth. And all around him was stone, stone, stone. The wildman's scream rent the sky. People down in the village crossed themselves and looked fearfully to the heavens.

At his scream two strange hairless men rushed down into the stone place; they were covered with flaps of some smooth stuff and held pointed things in their hands. Even in his own fear, he could smell their fear roiling off them, and it gave him a moment of calm. Enough to realise that this was the land that he could see from the sea, and that these were men who lived on the land as he lived in the sea. No point in being afraid. After that he was quiet, and he waited for them to take him back to where he belonged.

They brought him food, and he was hungry so he ate it, finding his hands hard to lift thanks to the heavy links. It tasted strange to him, flooding his mouth with the taste of the earth, but the taste was not unpleasant, so he welcomed the food. One of the landmen stayed with him. He was glad of that when night fell and the walls

of stone closed in on him until he could hardly breathe. But the landman gabbled at him constantly. He didn't understand that this was a language because his own was so very different.

At first they were friendly enough, even though they didn't take him to the sea or take off the heavy links. He began to accept that this was his life and the stone place wasn't so bad with the friendly landmen chattering at him. Sometimes they would bring him fish and his mouth would water. He took the fish and squeezed them as was right and proper so that all the water was gone and only the meat left and then ate them with relish, as they tasted of the sea and reminded him of his home.

Sometimes at night when the banging and shouting and clamour of the day had ceased he could hear the sea, and it called to him.

Then one day they took him with rough hands, and they tied him with ropes and they hung him upside down so that his blood ran to his head and made him dizzy, and then they started to whack his feet with a pole. The shock and the pain made him scream, and he didn't understand. It was the two landsmen who stayed with him and kept him safe. Were they not his friends? Why were they shouting at him? Why were they hurting him?

They beat him until he could no longer scream, just whimper, and then they took him down and threw him back in his corner.

Then they brought food but he turned from it and pressed his cheek against the cold stone.

'It's no good if he can't talk,' cried de Glanville. 'Who's to know he's not just some mute from this godforsaken back-of-beyond? If he's to be a prize for King Henry, then he must talk.'

The guards looked at each other. How the Wildman had screamed when they'd beaten him!

'My lord, I'm not sure he can talk,' said the younger one, John. 'But perhaps if he is given to God, then that might free his tongue.'

'Very well,' said de Glanville, turning away. 'Take him to the new church and see if the Lord changes him.'

So the Wildman was taken out of the dungeons and led through the building site, past the new walls that were creeping up around the keep and out into the village. John and Geoffrey, the older guard, led him towards the new, still-roofless church with its half-done nave that stood away from the castle. As soon as they were out, the Wildman turned and stared at the sea, and began to make gaping motions with his mouth.

'He wants to go home, poor sod,' said Geoffrey. He gave a tug on the chains that bound the Wildman. 'Not today, my lad. Today you're meeting God.'

They led him inside the church and up to the altar, genuflecting as they went. The Wildman did not bow, but he cooed when the sunlight struck the altar cross and made it glitter, and he ran the soft altar cloth through his hands. They showed him the freshly painted saints on the chancel walls, but he didn't seem to recognise even that they were images of men; he just stroked the colours and stared at the paint that came off on his webbed fingers. Once outside again, he pulled towards the sea. That night he wouldn't touch his food.

John and Geoffrey went back to de Glanville and said they feared for the Wildman if he was not allowed the sea.

De Glanville, afraid that his prize might die, said, 'You may let him go in the sea – so long as you ensure that he doesn't escape.'

A complex rigging of nets was lowered into the sea, weighted at the bottom to touch the ocean floor. The whole village turned out to see the spectacle, including Osmer and Eric. They watched as the Wildman was led into the corral. His chains were taken off and before anyone could do anything he had plunged underwater, and the next they knew he was on the other side of the nets swimming far out to sea. The villagers stared as he jumped up out of the water and then dived back down. He did this over and over, getting further and further out, and all were sure they'd lost him and he was parading like this just to mock them.

After a while, the sea was still, and people started to turn away. John and Geoffrey steeled themselves for their punishment, but then Osmer Hart called out, 'He's back!'

Sure enough, the Wildman was swimming once more in the little corral and looking very pleased with himself. That night he ate heartily of the roast beef they gave him as a treat, and at sunset he lay down to sleep as he always did.

Every day for two months he was taken down to the sea, and every evening he returned. All the while de Glanville plotted to get the King there to see his prize, but, though Henry was here, there and everywhere, he never came into Suffolk.

At the end of two months they let the Wildman take his swim as always, trusting that he would return as he always had, but that day they waited in vain. He was never seen again in Orford, and de Glanville never got his prize. But sometimes, when fishermen are far out to sea, they swear they can see someone waving at them from across the waves, and they know that the Wildman is still out there.

'The Wildman of Orford' is another story from Ralph de Coggeshall. Although the Wildman comes from the sea, he isn't a merman as we would usually imagine. He is more like the woodwoses that were supposed to live in wild places, covered in hair and totally lacking in civilisation. The earliest hairy man was Enkidu, the wild friend of Gilgamesh in the Sumerian epic, who like all wildmen, lived in nature and was part of nature. Coggeshall's Wildman is unusual in being from the sea, but is still hairy. Perhaps he is honoured on Orford's font, which has four woodwoses on it.

TWENTY-NINE

THE
DAUNTLESS GIRL

There were four farmers in Lavenham who liked to drink together of an evening. Instead of trusting themselves to a publican, they preferred to get some ale in and meet in each other's houses. The most popular destination was Walter Utteridge's house, just behind the church on Potland Road. Utteridge wasn't married, so there was no gimlet-eyed wife checking the level of the liquor, just his old housekeeper and a girl. The girl was, it must be confessed, the other reason the farmers liked to come to Utteridge's. Mary was a handsome, well-made girl. Not pretty, no. But she was bold and had a sharp, witty tongue on her. Whenever she came in the room the conversation ceased; and only started up again when she left.

That night Utteridge had miscalculated the amount of ale he and his friends would drink, and they were eyeing the last jug with alarm.

'Mary'll get more,' he said, and called for the girl. He instructed her to go to the Greyhound and no other pub. 'We'll know if you go elsewhere, so mark that you don't.'

She took the jug without a word and marched out into the night.

'I wonder which way she'll go,' said Toby Oxberry, swirling the dregs in his cup.

The quickest way to the Greyhound Inn on the High Street in the daytime was across the churchyard through the path at the back, and then out onto Church Street and up the hill.

'She's a girl!' cried Henry Coker. 'She'll never go that way.'

'Want to bet?' said the last member of the party, John Winthrop.

So the bets were laid. Utteridge, Oxberry and Winthrop said she would go through the churchyard, and Coker said she would go along Hall Road.

Eventually Mary came back and set the new jug down on the table.

'Now, Mary,' said Utteridge, 'which way did you go?'

Mary gave him a look. 'Through the churchyard, of course. It's the quickest way.'

Coker left the house a poorer man than he had come.

A week passed before the men met again. Coker was determined that he would get his money back, so it was a man with a plan who made his way to Utteridge's farm that night.

'You all think Mary's so dauntless, but I tell you she's not so bold.'

The men were interested when Coker outlined his idea. They agreed it was a fine plan, and the bets were laid exactly as it had been the week before, with only Coker denying Mary's boldness.

Mary was called in. Utteridge cleared his throat.

'Now, Mary, I've got a task for you. You've to go to the church, into the bonehouse, and bring us back a skull.'

Mary gave him a very long look at that, but she said nothing, just whirled on her cloak, took the rushlight from the wall and left. Fool idea, she thought. But then she thought, 'The church'll be locked and that'll be the end of it.' It was a quick walk to the church, and she thought she'd be as quickly home.

But the church was open.

So in she went. The moonlight streamed through the windows and cast long shadows across the tall arches, but Mary hardly noticed. The door to the crypt was open, so down she went into the darkness.

The rushlight gave only a dim, flickering light, but it was enough to see she was in a bonehouse. Four bare skulls grinned at her.. Mary reached for the nearest.

Immediately an eldritch voice shrieked out, 'No, not my father!'

She flinched back. But she had been sent on an errand, and she was not going back empty-handed. So she reached for the next one.

'No, not my mother!'

Well now. Her lips thinned. She reached again.

'Not my brother!'

At the end of her patience, she cried, 'Father, mother, brother or sister, it don't signify! I must have a skull,' and she grabbed the last skull and raced up the steps.

But as she neared the top a figure loomed out of the darkness beside her, all swirling white with black, black eyes. Mary didn't even react; she just shoved the skull under her arm rugby-style and barrelled her way out, banging the crypt door shut behind her.

When she got back to the farmhouse she smacked the skull down on the table and said, 'There it is, and I hope you profit by it!'

But they would not let her go; they made her tell the whole tale, and when she got to the part about pushing past the ghost and shutting it in the bonehouse, Henry Coker went very pale.

'Ahem,' he said. 'I think it might be wise to go down to the church.'

So the four farmers went to the church with their big candle lanterns. They found the church in silence and the bonehouse door shut. But when they opened the door they saw that on the stairs lay a figure wrapped in a large white sheet with two holes cut out of it. When they pulled the sheet away they saw it was the old verger, Thomas Death. And dead he was.

'What's this, Coker?' said Utteridge.

And Coker was forced to reveal his plan. 'I bribed old Death here to open up the church,' he said. 'He was to scare the girl so I'd win my bet, but it looks like she scared him.'

After the trial, everyone said Coker was lucky to get away with a caution.

Mary found it hard to be in Lavenham after that. The looks and the whispers were just too much. When the opportunity of a job at the Hall at Long Melford came she snapped it up.

This was no ordinary job, though. Well, the job itself was an ordinary enough maid's job, definitely a cut above where she had been before, but not unusual. It was the circumstances that were tricksy. The squire just could not keep a girl in the job. He explained the reason at the interview.

'Ever since my mother died she's been haunting the place. She terrorises the girls; I don't know why. We've tried to get the priest to lay her, but she just won't go. So the position's yours if you think you can handle it. They say that you are that dauntless girl from Lavenham way.'

Mary allowed that she was from Lavenham, and she took the job.

The old mother soon made herself known. She liked to come to meals and make the squire's fine knives and forks fly about. Mary had a solution for that. When she was called to wait at the table, she always made sure that a place was laid for the ghost, and while the meal was taking place she would serve the ghost as if she was there, putting meat and vegetables on her plate and filling up her glass.

The ghost quietened, and the Hall seemed an easier place.

Then, one night, as Mary was sleeping in her attic room, she felt a presence in the room and opened her eyes. Standing at the end of the bed stood a tall old woman dressed in old-fashioned clothes and looking back at her. Nothing too unusual, except that the woman glowed with an unearthly light and Mary could see right through her.

'You know who I am, don't you, Mary?' said the apparition.

'That I do,' said Mary. 'You're the old madam.'

'Are you afraid of me, Mary?'

Mary shook her head. 'Not me, madam; the reason being that I'm alive and you're dead.'

The figure gave a gaunt smile.

'You are a dauntless one, aren't you? Well, you'll do. Come along then.'

Mary got out of bed and followed the old lady down the stairs to the cellars.

'Move those bricks,' said the ghost.

Mary saw that where she pointed in the corner of the room there were some loose bricks. When she moved them two sacks were revealed, one large and one small.

'Open them.'

Inside the sacks were great piles of shining gold.

'The large sack is for my son – the taxman won't get it now. And the small sack is for you, as you've been such a dauntless girl.'

With that the old lady vanished, leaving Mary in the darkness. Well, she hauled those sacks back up to her attic, and she thought about it, and the more she thought, the more unfair it seemed. The squire already had this fine house and all the fine things in it, and plenty of land and money beside, so why should he get the large sack? Mary decided that she would try her luck.

The next day she went to the squire, with the sacks, and she told him what had happened, from the old lady coming to her bedside to the discovery of the sacks. 'And she said that the small was for you, and the large one was for me, because I was such a dauntless girl.'

The squire was astonished to hear that his mother would cheat him so, but you didn't gainsay a ghost. He pondered all day and all night over what her message to him might be. Should he be living more frugally? Was it a punishment for some childhood deed?

Was he not brave enough? That led him to thinking about Mary. She was a handsome girl, he thought. Not pretty, no. But she was well made, and that bold tongue entranced him. Or so he told himself.

So he married her, and thus got all the money. And Mary got fine clothes and a fancy house and all the things she could have wanted. But there was little love between them after a year or two. He took to drinking and he beat her. And Mary wondered to herself in dark moments whether there was a possibility that she had been too bold, as it never does to cross a ghost.

'The Dauntless Girl' is well known in East Anglia, with versions from both Suffolk and Norfolk. The earliest version is a Norfolk one, from Walter Rye's Recreations of a Norfolk Antiquary, 1920, but it also has a strong tradition in the far south-western corner of Suffolk and is known from Justin and Edith Brooke's Suffolk Prospect, which draws on tales from before World War II. There isn't a crypt in Lavenham now, but there really was a Thomas Death who lived there in the early 1700s.

THIRTY

THE GHOST WHO CARED TOO MUCH

It was past midnight, but a light still burnt in the window of the Queen's Head in Blyford. The landlord hefted a bottle from the top shelf and carried it over to his table.

'Doctor says I should drink less,' he said. 'But what she don't know won't hurt her.'

'Too right,' said old Jim, the only other occupant of the bar. 'One drink won't kill us – not tonight, bor.'

The landlord sat down and poured two large measures of whisky, and was just reaching for his glass when suddenly the temperature plummeted. The bottle floated into the air, hung there for a moment and then smashed against the wall. The heady scent of whisky filled the room. Belatedly, the landlord and old Jim scraped back their chairs and stepped away from the table.

As they stood and stared, the landlord's full glass slid off the table and crashed to the floor.

For a long moment, all was silent save for the drip, drip of whisky from the wall. Then the landlord said, 'You know what that is, Jim? That's Eloise making trouble again.'

Eloise was well known to the landlord. It was said she'd once been the landlady of the pub, and she'd just ... stayed. Echoes of the past were everywhere in the Queen's Head. The sound of running footsteps on the stairs to the cellar when there was no one there, sharp cracking sounds, certain areas that were cold even with the heating at full whack, a glimpse of a shadowy figure in long skirts. Once, a couple of guests in the upstairs room had reported waking early – 4.22 a.m., their mobiles said – and found the room absolutely freezing. When the landlord investigated, he discovered that the heating – which should have been running all that cold night – had gone off. The timer had been set to turn off at 4.22 a.m. Someone had even spotted an old man wearing what was described as a 'pirate hat, you know, with three corners'. He was running up the cellar stairs – before he disappeared.

There was a bricked-up opening in the cellar which everyone knew was a secret tunnel to the church next door. Smugglers, people said, and winked. It was said there was a bricked-up opening by the altar in the church, too. It was a joke, but the landlord and his wife had to live with it, and by now they were familiar with Eloise, the running man and the cold. But this trick with the whisky took the biscuit.

It was Eloise's mission to keep the Queen's Head safe. If the landlord had been told by his doctor he shouldn't drink, then she wouldn't let him harm himself. She would look after him. She'd been trying to look after the place for nigh on two hundred years. It hadn't always worked. The terrible fire in 1988 had caused her great grief. Since then she'd stepped up her efforts. The Queen's Head had to be safe, because Eloise never forgot that she had failed those she had sworn to protect.

When Eloise took over the pub, she'd only been there a couple of weeks when, late one night when she was heading to the privy, someone stepped out of the shadows and grabbed her.

'Quiet now,' he said, and she felt the prick of a dagger against her throat. 'Don't move, 'cos I'd not want anything to happen to that pretty neck o' yours. There's something you need to know: you're working for the Dunwich gang now.'

He told her the pub was a smuggler's safe house. Goods would appear in her cellar, and she'd better turn a blind eye, or else there'd be trouble. She obeyed. She learnt who the Revenue men were. She set a light in the left-hand window if all was clear and one in the right if the Revenue men were there.

That Saturday night was a busy one and Eloise was rushed off her feet. She was alone in the pub, but when the message came that she might be expecting late visitors she whipped upstairs and lit the left-hand light. But just as she was closing up a posse of Revenue men stepped inside and sat themselves down. The leader was John Cook, a man she knew well for his casual cruelty.

'It's closing time, lads,' she said. 'Better make it a swift one.'

Cook shook his head.

'It's not closing time for us, Eloise. We're going to make ourselves comfortable here until those visitors of yours come.'

The window! Eloise had to move the light to let the smugglers know. When she tried to leave, Cook was up like a shot. He clamped his hand on her wrist.

'We needs our lovely Eloise serving drinks to us down here. So don't you think about going nowhere. You're with us tonight.'

The light still burned. There was nothing she could do.

In Dunwich young Todd Larter was up the tower of All Saints' Church, watching the sea. Every year the church crept closer to the edge of the cliff, and its loneliness made it the perfect lookout. Every time he went up there, he strained to hear the bells of the old city ringing under the waves. Sometimes he thought he heard them, but not that night. He wasn't up there long. There was the flash, flash of the lantern from the dark sea, then Todd was scrambling down the crumbling steps, and racing down the cliff and across the harbour to where Matthias Swan was waiting. The two of them made their way together along the Dingle path.

At the meeting point was the third member of their party, Old Bill. He was taking his ease on an overturned boat on the edge of the marsh, smoking his pipe. Bill cocked his old-fashioned tricorne at them, then gestured with his pipe to where the boat was approaching the shore.

'Revenue are out tonight, watching the mouth of the Blyth,' he said. 'We're over-landing, boys.'

A line of patient packhorses were waiting. With a few muttered greetings, the men loaded up the kegs from the boat when it pulled in, and then set out across the marsh.

'We'll stash the barrels at Blyford tonight,' said Matthias.

'Should we take the Walks?' asked Todd.

'Revenue are sure to be there,' said Bill. 'But we can cut across Toby's Walks up to Blythburgh. No Revenue man'll stay there of a night!'

After that there was no talking. The three men walked along the edge of the Dingle marsh and across the Westwood meadows, keeping to the shadowy tracks. They skirted Lumphall Walks, then shot as fast as the horses would go across to Toby's Walks, where the gibbet still swung.

'I was just a nipper when that 'un was hanged,' whispered Bill as they crept under the grisly cage. 'That Black Toby was a rakehell and a murderer. They do say his spirit walks here on dark nights like this.'

'I never seen anything here, save for rabbits!' laughed Matthias.

Todd clutched his horse's lead rein harder and stared at the ground until they were safe away.

After Toby's Walks it was a short hop to Blythburgh and the river. Nestled in a thicket overhanging the stream was a small rowing boat. The three men loaded the kegs from the horses into the boat. Todd led the horses to the yard of the White Hart, secured them, then ran back to the boat.

They were on their guard as they set off up the navigation, each man with his pistol cocked in case of the Revenue. At the tidal staunch the lockkeeper let them through. He received a small keg as a reward. Then it was plain sailing until Blyford Bridge.

They moored up and then began the slow process of manhandling the kegs up to the church. Matthias nodded at the light burning in the left window of the Queen's Head.

'All clear,' he said.

By the time they had piled the kegs into the tunnel between church and pub and rolled them to the door into Queen's Head's cellar it was past four in the morning.

At twenty past four the bar was shrouded in darkness save for the dim glow of the fire. The Revenue men sat in silence. Cook still had his hand clamped over Eloise's arm. Into the silence came a strange rumbling noise from below. Eloise closed her eyes in defeat. The Revenue men leapt up. Cook clapped a hand over Eloise's mouth.

'Remember, round here *we're* the law, so you keep your pretty mouth shut or there'll be trouble.'

He shoved her away and followed his men to the cellar steps.

Meanwhile, Todd came into the cellar, a brandy keg clutched against his chest. He was just about to put it down when the door above burst open and down the steps ran the Revenue men, pistols waving. Todd was so shocked he could only stand and stare, all too aware that he damned himself by what he held. Matthias knocked past him into the cellar.

'What you dawdling for, bor?' Then he too stopped. 'Christ! We've bin betrayed.'

In horror, Todd saw him draw his pistol.

'Drop it if you want to live!' called Cook.

'Eloise, you're damned for this!' cried Matthias.

Then he fired. A cracking shot rang out and a revenue man dropped. Even as he fell, the others started shooting. Matthias gave a grunt, and Todd saw him crumple. That unfroze him, and he flung himself to one side. Too late. Sudden shocking pain blossomed in his chest. He fell. The keg crashed to the floor and the scent of brandy filled the air. His vision fogged, and the pain squeezed him, but at the top of the stairs he saw Eloise, haloed by a candle flame, tears streaming down her face.

'Damn you!' he whispered. His world went black.

Eloise saw the boy sag and closed her eyes. Matthias was already dead. How could this happen in her pub? Then, as the Revenue were congratulating themselves, another figure burst from the gloom and ran up the steps, tricorne bouncing on his head. Old Bill. Before the Revenue could react, he was through the door and away.

The Revenue found forty kegs stashed along the tunnel. During the next few days, men came to brick up the entrance. Eloise stood by and let them. After that, she was a shadow of her former self. She could no longer serve in the bar. All her life she was convinced she had failed to protect the smugglers, and failed the pub as well.

For two hundred years she guarded the place. After she died her spirit kept alive the memory of that night. The landlord, like those before him, got used to the haunting.

One night a nurse at the hospital in Halesworth was having a drink, when she sensed something … unhappy. She went to the landlord and asked if she could try to speak to the spirit. He was retiring in a month and was happy to give his assent. The nurse went into the room where Eloise was known to sit, and spoke to her. When she was done she went back to the landlord.

'She wants to pass on,' said the nurse. 'But she's afraid of something. She worries for you. She kept saying that she had to protect the pub. I told her that you were fine and the pub was safe. Other people were watching it, I said. She seemed satisfied and I think she'll go, if we can guide her.'

The landlord spoke to the vicar to arrange a mass to exorcise the ghost. The vicar came and the words were said. The landlord wasn't sure what would happen, but the change was immediate. Those last four weeks in the job were the most peaceful he'd ever known. The pub felt completely different. He knew that Eloise was finally at rest.

Smuggling was rife all the way along the Suffolk coast from the seventeenth to the nineteenth centuries. It was a major and, to the ordinary folk, legitimate way of augmenting the poor wages of agricultural workers and fishermen. The trade must have supplied many restless spirits over the years to the coast and the nearby villages. Eloise may have been sent to her rest, but we can still tell the stories of the Blyford ghosts. And there are many more stories out there, just waiting to be told.

BIBLIOGRAPHY

Anon, *An Authentic History of Maria Marten; or, the Red Barn!* (London: Milner, n.d.)

Anon, *The Secret Disclosed: A Legend of St. Edmund's Abbey by an Inmate* (Bury St Edmunds: Samuel Gross, n.d.)

Anon, *The Lost Expedition*, www.lostexpedition.co.uk

Ashford, Ronald, *1940: The Secret War at Shingle Street*, http://www. shford.fslife.co.uk/ShingleSt/index.html

Barnardiston, K.W., *Clare Priory: Seven Centuries of a Suffolk House* (Cambridge: W. Heffer, 1962)

Bede, *Ecclesiastical History of the English People* (London: Penguin Books, 1990)

Birch, Mel, *Suffolk's Ancient Sites – Historic Places* (Mendlesham: Castell, 2004)

Briggs, Katherine M., *A Dictionary of British Folk-Tales in the English Language, Part A: Folk Narratives* (London: Routledge, 1990)

Brooke, Justin and Brooke, Edith, *Suffolk Prospect* (London: The Country Book Club, 1965)

Bunn, Ivan A.W. and Baker, Henry, *Haunted Lowestoft Revisited* (Lowestoft: privately published with help from Lowestoft Heritage Workshop Centre, 2010)

Burgess, Mike, *Hidden East Anglia*, www.hiddenea.com

Carey Evans, Margaret, *Hoxne and St Edmund* (Diss: BC Publications, 1995)

Clarke, Theo and Sinclair, Nick, *Ebb & Flow: River Heritage Walks* (Woodbridge: Suffolk Coastal District Council, 2008)

Dixon, G.M., *Folktales and Legends of Suffolk* (Deeping St James: Minimax Books, 1982)

Ellis, Robin R., 'The "Yerk" Bells' - Hidden England, www.hiddenengland. com.ar/yerkbells

Ford, James, The Suffolk Garland (Ipswich: J. Raw, 1818)

Forman, Joan, Haunted East Anglia (London: Robert Hale, 1976)

Frith, Roger, 'Dragons in Essex', (East Anglian Magazine, July 1962), pp. 522–524

Gylde, John, Jnr, The New Suffolk Garland (London: Simpkin, Marshall & Co., 1866)

Gurdon, Lady Eveline Camilla (ed.), County Folk-Lore Suffolk: Printed Extracts No. 2 Suffolk (London: The Folklore Society, 1893)

James, M.H., Bogie Tales of East Anglia (Ipswich: Pawsey & Hayes, 1891)

Jennings, Pete, Haunted Suffolk (Stroud: Tempus, 2006)

Knott, Simon, The Suffolk Churches Site, www.suffolkchurches.co.uk

Mann, Ethel, Old Bungay (London: Heath Cranton, 1934)

Matten, J.M., The Cult of St Edmund (Thurston: Drecroft, 1996)

Murdie, Alan, Haunted Bury St Edmunds (Stroud: Tempus, 2006)

Newton, Sam, The Reckoning of King Rædwald: The Story of the King Linked to the Sutton Hoo Ship-Burial (Brightlingsea: Red Bird Press, 2003)

Orriss, Margaret and Haining, Peter (eds), The Murder in the Red Barn (Ipswich: Polstead Community Shop, n.d.)

Out of This World Episode 3 (BBC1, 1996) [TV programme]

Plunkett, Steven, Suffolk in Anglo-Saxon Times (Stroud: Tempus, 2005)

Redstone, Vincent B. (ed.), Memorials of Old Suffolk (London: Bemrose, 1926)

Rose, Jack and Parkin, Dean, The Grit: The Story of Lowestoft's Beach Village (Lowestoft: Rushmere Publishing, 1998)

Sampson, Charles, The Ghosts of the Broads (Norwich: Jarrold, 1973)

Scarfe, Norman, The Suffolk Landscape (London: Hodder & Stoughton, 1972)

Scarfe, Norman, Suffolk in the Middle Ages (Woodbridge: Boydell Press, 2004)

Fison, Lois A., and Thomas, Mrs Walter, Merry Suffolk (London: Jarrold, 1899)

Thompson, Leonard P., The Smugglers of the Suffolk Coast (Hadleigh: Brett Valley, 1968)

Tongue, Ruth L., Forgotten Folk-Tales of the English Counties (London: Routledge & Kegan Paul, 1970)

Westwood, Jennifer and Simpson, Jacqueline, The Lore of the Land: A Guide to England's Legends, from Spring-Heeled Jack to the Witches of Warboys (London: Penguin Books, 2006)

INDEX